T0198592

IN SEARCH

OF THE

ANIMALCULE

Steven L. Berk, M.D.

IN SEARCH OF THE ANIMALCULE

iUniverse books may be ordered through booksellers or by contacting:

iUniverse
1663 Liberty Drive
Bloomington, IN 47403
www.iuniverse.com
844-349-9409

ISBN: 978-1-6632-4800-8 (sc)
ISBN: 978-1-6632-4801-5 (hc)
ISBN: 978-1-6632-4799-5 (e)

Library of Congress Control Number: 2022921645

Print information available on the last page.

iUniverse rev. date: 12/01/2022

As for the animalcules, it is a terrifying thought that life is at the mercy of these minute bodies. It is consoling that Science will not be powerless before such enemies.
—Louis Pasteur

CONTENTS

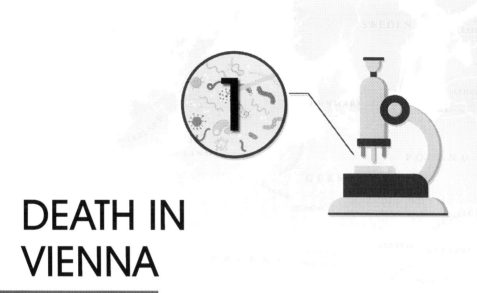

DEATH IN
VIENNA

I do not remember my mother, as we shared only two days on earth together. But one might say that my birth and her death set in place events that would change the world forever. The death of my mother would disclose a horrible secret and change the lives of men, women, and children over the coming centuries. And I, an orphan of little means, would be the catalyst for a revelation so great that no individual from any land would be unaffected. My name is Jacob Pfleger, and I was there to see the greatest breakthroughs in science and medicine ever known. My story begins with what happened to my mother and dozens of other women of her time. This is what I have been told.

My mother knew, within hours after my birth, that she was ill. And by dawn the next morning, after a restless sleep and the onset of feverishness and chills, she knew that she would be dead within days. My mother was no stranger to postpartum fever, for she was an obstetrician, one of the very few women obstetricians in Europe.

Death was no stranger to my mother, not in Vienna and not in the wards of the large, gratis Viennese maternity hospital Allgemeines Krankenhaus. But my mother, Theresa Marie Pfleger, vowed that she would not die with her secret, a dark, troubling secret that she shared with only a few of her male colleagues in this Vienna hospital in March 1847.

My mother's nurse, a coworker named Hannah Mandel, was also a close friend. Hannah held her in great esteem in a culture of chauvinism. So when Theresa Marie asked to have her mentor, teacher, and friend Professor Jakob Kolletschka summoned to her bedside, her nurse made every effort to oblige.

Kolletschka had always guided my mother, encouraging her through medical school, protecting her from the male-dominated hierarchy of academic medicine, and forewarning her of the Habsburg Empire's window of opportunity in education and science. Kolletschka was known by the entire physician community as a distinguished forensic pathologist, the one who would conduct the autopsy and have the answer to why any patient had died. Kolletschka had become a sharer of the secret.

Hannah found it impossible to find or contact Kolletschka. Appearing at my mother's bedside instead was Josef Skoda, a colleague and sharer of the secret. Skoda, with his long, straight brown hair, spectacles, green bow tie, and brown three-piece suit, his jacket close to touching the white hospital floor, looked down upon her with shame. The founder of the Vienna Medical School and a brilliant professor who gave his lectures in Latin, he was intelligent enough to be a sharer of the secret but not the man who would battle the status quo. His colorful clothing pierced the room's sea of white—the white wooden walls of the hospital, the white uniforms, and the white hooded caps of the nurses. Today my mother's pale skin appeared whiter than ever. She ignored the sounds of nearby women crying out in the midst of labor, ignored the vague smell of urine—all just part of a public hospital.

She grimaced when she saw Josef. Josef Skoda was a good and kind man, an accomplished professor and obstetrician. But he was a man of science and a man of few words, more comfortable writing than speaking, perhaps not the right man to be at the deathbed of an esteemed colleague.

"Josef, I asked for Jakob, not you."

"Theresa Marie, I must suffice. But Division One! That was not the plan. That was not the ward you were to be assigned to. Absurd. How could you have the delivery in Division One and by Dr. Braun of all choices—you, who first noted the dangers of Division One? Dr. Braun, who frequently shuttles between the delivery ward and the autopsy room, has completely rejected our concerns about these deliveries."

"Foolish Josef, I had no choice—it was Saturday. Your anger directed at me is just the frustration that we all share. My midwife had promised to be available when the time came, but I was two weeks early, and she was in Budapest. You and Ignaz—perhaps I should have tried to find you. But Dr. Braun is who they called. He smiled and told me that he had not been in the laboratory. I was in pain, and of course, I was frightened—my first baby. So I did not argue with fate's choice of my obstetrician. And my civility, perhaps, will become my fatal mistake. But I must speak with Kolletschka."

And then she knew, for Josef Skoda also was the protégé of Jakob Kolletschka. Josef was not a man of emotion or great sensitivity, so when Theresa Marie saw a tear in the eye of this man of science, a man who had witnessed the deaths of newborns and mothers without expression, she knew that another tragedy was upon her.

Josef did not need to answer, for while he was carefully, slowly, and awkwardly choosing his words, the other members of the team—obstetricians, fellow faculty, the other holders of Vienna's deadly secret—also arrived at the bedside of my dying mother. With curtains drawn and small wooden guest chairs arranged around the cement slab of my mother's bed, Josef Skoda and the two new arrivals—other members of the obstetrics team, Ferdinand von Hebra and Ignaz Semmelweis—stared at my mother with a grief too extraordinary for words. But none of them could adequately capture the pathos of the moment.

Hebra hugged my mother and kissed her hand. He was a young man, no older than she was. Of the three at the bedside, he was the most articulate, emotional, and potentially persuasive. "Theresa Marie, it's a blessing that you have a healthy son, but that you are ill is heartbreaking." He began to sob for the inevitable and ironic fate of my mother.

Josef looked at Semmelweis and Hebra. "She has asked about Kolletschka."

Theresa Marie already knew by then that he must be dead.

"Our cherished friend, our mentor—suddenly, tragically," whispered Semmelweis. He spoke in a Hungarian dialect, identifying himself as an outsider. He hid behind a large, thick black mustache turned upward at each end and had large eyes and black hair that was prematurely balding. He wore a sad look.

Ignaz Semmelweis had been born to a Hungarian family of limited means, his father a grocer, and in Vienna his dialect was a source of amusement. A man of genius but with limited interpersonal skills, he looked at my mother with a sense of guilt, despair, and anger but also resolve. For five years Semmelweis had been a colleague of my mother's, hired to be a hospital obstetrician by the more senior Skoda. He soon had developed a reputation as a Hungarian "liberal" with radical views on science and medicine. But he had been appointed chief of obstetrics, and the outcomes of the women in all the wards were thus his responsibility.

"Marie, Kolletschka cut his finger during an autopsy the day before yesterday," Semmelweis said hesitantly. "At first it was just a cut, but then redness and pain developed. The inflammation spread quickly. Fever, chills, low blood pressure, delirium, and death followed. He died at home, knowing there was not much to be done. His own autopsy was completed today."

My mother was horrified but also anticipated the importance of what was to come.

"The same changes—the same inflammation, meningitis, liver changes, lymphangitis, pneumonia," said Semmelweis. "The causes of deaths for the women in Division One and for Kolletschka are one and the same. I now see clearly that the disease from which he died is identical to that of our maternity patients. I will always be haunted by his death."

"And mine?" added my mother.

And so huddled around my mother's deathbed, the group again expressed that their worst fears were coming true, and their secret, their frightening suspicion, could no longer be contained. It was no surprise that even my courageous mother had been hesitant to speak out, for they were proposing an idea to explain the deaths of the childbearing women of Vienna that would enrage the medical community, devastate the families of so many women who had died at childbirth, and turn powerful and respected individuals into enemies.

My mother began to have a shaking chill, and her face became flushed. But there was little even this group of physicians could do— prevent such a disease, perhaps, but the possibility of curing it was a hundred years away in time.

As the group rose to give Theresa Marie her chance to rest, my mother asked Ignaz to stay a moment longer.

"Ignaz, you must end this scourge tomorrow. Too many women dying in Ward One."

"There is no longer any doubt," said Ignaz Semmelweis. "The irony is that the death of Kolletschka proves the point. The cause of death is the same particles, the same toxin."

"And you have checked all other possibilities?"

"Marie, have we not been through this so many times before? Like what possibilities? The seasons, the bad air? Absurd. There is no other logical conclusion."

"Then I ask you to promise me that tomorrow it will end."

"Yes, this, for you, for all women, I promise."

"I will ask you again. This poison on the hands of the doctors— why does it produce some of the same symptoms that I have seen in typhus, in consumption?"

"You know you ask about things that we have no knowledge of."

"And one last fear, Ignaz: do you know of the work of the Dutchman, Leeuwenhoek?"

"He was a businessman, Marie, and his work is discredited."

"Yes, but the idea—the small animals, too small to be seen except by microscope. Could they be the true poison?"

"The animalcules! Who would believe such an idea? Poison on our hands from the autopsy room is unbelievable enough!"

"Yes, perhaps so. My feet, feel them. They have been warm to the touch."

"They are cold, Marie. They are very cold."

"My time is now very precious. So, Ignaz, a second promise. My boy—I will call him Jacob after Kolletschka—he will be placed in the academy orphanage where I was raised. It was redemptive for me and will suffice for him. He will grow up as I did with resilience and independence."

"Your husband, Marie?"

"Yes, my husband. Well, a Viennese doctor should not marry a French wine merchant. He is in Lille. He knew of the pregnancy and chose not to return. He will be of no use to my son, Ignaz. He was a mistake, a moment's indiscretion. My son will grow up strong without him, without me. In this I have great faith. But I want him to know about our thoughts, our secret, our mistake, and our amends. When he is old enough—twelve, perhaps—you and Hebra, tell him our story. So that is a second promise you will have to keep."

"Yes, a promise that I can also keep."

And by the next morning, my mother, like thousands of other women in Vienna and around the world, had died of childbed fever.

A REVELATION AND PROMISE KEPT

The Vienna General Hospital was divided into two wards. Each maternity ward delivered several thousand babies per year. In Ward One, all deliveries were done by obstetricians; in Ward Two, by midwives. When it came to normal deliveries, all the practitioners were very capable. But in Ward One, there were six hundred deaths per year, ten times higher than the mortality rate in the midwife ward. Transfers from one ward to another might have obscured these differences, but to those who practiced in the hospital, it was clear that something was seriously wrong. After all, many women gave birth at home, and such deliveries were not considered dangerous.

Vienna was not a backward city as regards medical care. On the contrary, it was the center for new ideas and a renaissance city for breakthroughs in the understanding of pathology. In Vienna, physicians were likely to better understand the deaths of their patients by reviewing the autopsies conducted in the morgue, or even by going from morgue to patient in clinics or in the hospital.

The day after my mother died, there was a new testament to her life. Standing between the two wards was a large, round, white stone basin filled with chlorine. It had been put there because it finally had to be. It was there in tribute to my mother. It was there to end the scourge of Vienna. It was there so science could prevail. It was there to reveal the secret of why there had been so much death and misery in Ward One of the Vienna maternity wards.

Semmelweis, who was in charge of Ward One, put in place an ordinance that required every physician to wash his hands in an aqueous solution of the chloride of lime, an agent that made utensils clean, rid the hands of odors that came from the formalin-filled cadavers, and was meant to destroy those postulated toxic particles that Kolletschka had accidently injected into his skin, the same particles that had killed my mother.

But science is not so simple, and human nature breeds jealousy, intransigence, and skepticism. I think my mother would have understood the rage that her fellow practitioners around the country and around Europe displayed in reaction to the Semmelweis edict. That one's own hands might be responsible for the deaths of so many women was beyond comprehension to most. Toxic particles on the hands of the best doctors in Europe causing the death of women—the idea was as incongruous as a flat earth or a central sun.

Mother's friend Ferdinand von Hebra, a great writer and communicator, wrote in a medical journal several months later, "This most important discovery worthy of being placed besides Jenner's discovery of cowpox inoculation has been completely confirmed in the local maternity hospital, and supporting testimonials have been received from foreign countries."

Semmelweis and Hebra told their story and preached their gospel. Year after year, they explained what no one, not even the great minds of the Habsburg of Europe, had known. They spoke of death-causing particles, too small to be seen, rapidly ending the lives of the previously healthy.

Personal attacks against Hebra and especially against Semmelweis came swiftly, continuously, and with ferocity. Semmelweis had never been well-liked in Vienna. He was foreign-born and spoke in a dialect that made him seem uneducated. Some criticism was based on alternate scientific hypotheses. Hand washing had decreased the incidence of childbed fever where it was tried, but some cases, even in the Vienna General Hospital, still occurred. Childbed fever did occur, although rarely, on the streets of Vienna and in homes around Europe. Dr. Carl Braun, a practitioner in the Vienna Ward One, spoke of the many women who came to deliver and were already ill with pneumonia and meningitis even before being examined.

But most importantly, Braun and others could not accept these toxic particles as a reality—particles that could not be seen or felt but only smelled, particles that caused inflammation and spread to all parts of the body as if they were alive, leaving severe pathologic changes in the liver, heart, and blood vessels.

Semmelweis did not manage the criticism well. Had my mother survived, he might have been directed by her gentle hand in his debate, but left to his own devices, he became bitter, loud, and passionate. While the debate was raging, Ignaz's term as ward director came to an end. He saw his opponents as murderers. And so only a few years after his successful intervention in the wards of the Vienna hospital where my mother had died, he was fired.

To his leading opponent, Dr. Joseph Spaeth, an influential and well-respected professor and obstetrician, he wrote, "Herr Professor, you have convinced me that the Puerperal Sun that arose in Vienna in the year 1847 has not enlightened your mind although it shone so near to you. This arrogant ignoring of my doctrine demands that I make the following declaration. Within myself, I bear the knowledge that since the year 1847, thousands and thousands of puerperal women have died who would not have died had I not kept silent. And you, Herr Professor, have been my partner in the massacre. The murder must cease, and in order for it to cease, I will keep watch, and anyone who dares to propagate dangerous errors about childbed fever will find in me an eager adversary. In order to put an end to these murders I have no recourse but to mercilessly expose my adversaries."

To Friedrich Scanzoni, a leading German professor of obstetrics, Semmelweis stated, "Should you, Herr Professor, without having disproved my doctrine continue to train your pupils in the doctrine of epidemic fever, I declare before God and the world that you are a murderer." I often wondered whether his passion stemmed not only from the death of many amorphous faces but also from the one death that he could not forget, that of his familiar colleague.

Hebra and Skoda never doubted Semmelweis, nor would have my deceased mother. But Skoda soon lost interest in the battle, having made great contributions in other areas of medicine, and Hebra was too genteel for this debate, writing about childbed fever convincingly but parting ways from the disturbed Semmelweis.

Ignaz Semmelweis became more stressed and debilitated. Tired and frustrated, he asked to meet with Hebra as he prepared to leave Vienna forever.

Hebra, who had not seen his colleague for years, was shocked at his appearance. Tired, gray, and disheveled, his friend appeared thoroughly defeated.

"I have done my best to change the thinking of my colleagues, and I have tried to end the scourge of puerperal fever at least in the Vienna General Hospital. But there is a second promise to be fulfilled," said Semmelweis.

And so, twelve years after my mother's death, with the debate about childbed fever still raging, Hebra and Semmelweis began their search for me.

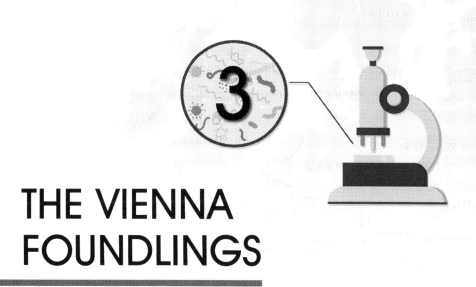

THE VIENNA
FOUNDLINGS

My mother had been an orphan herself, having been abandoned in the same hospital wards where she would later practice medicine. Her story was a common one: left at birth by a young mother, poor and without means to raise a child. My mother's childhood home had become the Vienna Foundlings and Orphans Home, located just across the street from the hospital itself. Those children who survived childhood by escaping death from pneumonia or malnutrition were subjected to a rigorous regimen of discipline, chores, meager rations, and solitude. But there were books and studies and, on occasion, great ideas and inspirations.

I spent twelve years in the Vienna Foundlings. To some it was the worst place on earth, but it was all that we had and all that we knew. Middle-aged women who acted as foster mothers, extremely poor themselves, tried to care for us in two daily shifts. They would come and go frequently, and today I would not remember the names of any of them. There were children of all types: those like me, moved from the Vienna Maternity Hospital after birth and cared for by volunteers, but also street children moved by the court system from juvenile prisons to our home for rehabilitation, as well as children who were disabled—blind, deaf, and deformed. For most, it was open sleeping quarters, regular eating hours, and multiple chores, and for some, there were special classes. Those like me who could learn to read had access to the library resource and plenty of desks and good lighting. Two boys, Neil and Gedeon, had been friends for as long as I could remember. Like me they asked questions and wondered what was outside the walls of our institution and what special fate was in store for us. The townsfolk were charitable, and the home had adequate food, cheese, bread, fruits, and vegetables for us. I remember Neil with his brown hair hanging over his forehead to his eyes, his white tunic down stretching past his waist, and his knickerbocker pants reaching his knees. As with all of us, his clothes had belonged to at least two or three children before him and never quite fit. Neil seemed to be a few years older than I was. He had begun his growth spurt, giving him an awkwardness in speech and gait. Gedeon was about the same age as Neil but had a more rebellious nature, as reflected in his long black hair that he was loath to cut, his black cap tilted over one eye, and his black boots, which were more military style than our short, soft boots and which a visiting soldier had given him.

Several events stand out among my years of austere existence at the orphanage: the meeting with my headmaster at age ten, the winter of death, the outbreak of the red-face disease, and the surprise physician visitors.

It was a usual classroom session with about twenty boys and girls reading a simple text about growing up in Vienna. I had learned to read at an early age, about age four, with the help of a dedicated school room volunteer and with the advantage of a library that held books of all types and all levels of difficulty. I read everything I could find that would help describe the world, the philosophy of why we were alive, the works of philosophers, the Bible, and Greek mythology. I chose not to share this with my teachers because I had heard I could be moved to a different place altogether for knowing or learning too much.

One day, one of the youngest boys had done nothing to prepare for his lessons, and our teacher became frustrated and angry. "Son, you are surely going to be a nobody without an education and without parents, without a proper upbringing. You are bound for hell."

This condemnation of the boy moved me to tears and an emotional state that I had always tried to avoid, and at that moment I was compelled to respond and defend the child.

"Sir, you do not train a child to learn by force or harshness but direct them to it by what amuses their minds, so that you may be better able to discover with accuracy their peculiar talent."

"Jacob, where in heaven did you find those words?"

"Sir, they are the words of Plato."

"And you have memorized the works of Plato?"

"I have read the words, and most often, what I read, I retain."

It was because of this interchange that I became a child of interest. A mathematician with the University of Vienna showed me many different shapes and asked me to determine the angles of such shapes, especially triangles. I found such exercises to be of no interest. A member of Vienna's chess society taught me how to play the game, and I was quite adept at it, easily triumphing over most of the adult members. It seemed that I was able to predict quite easily the moves of my opponent, but again I found no interest in pursuing this pastime. I even spent time with a piano teacher but had little talent for music. In the end I was accepted as a child who only wanted to read and study, who could memorize what he read and was content to pursue an understanding of the world and the rules that govern it as he searched for his role in it.

A few years later, the responsibility came upon Neil, Gedeon, and me, our being among the most able-bodied and mentally alert of all the children in the unit, to care for the sick during the winter of 1858. It was a very cold winter, and it was a particularly crowded time for the orphanage, with more soldiers going to war against our neighboring countries and many couples leaving Austria for better, more peaceful lives.

Neil was the individual who would read and study with me. He was always willing to care for the children and to learn about the great Austrian scientists. But Neil was an orphan who had no interest in who his parents were, where he came from, or where he was going. He had experienced more abuse than most of us. Gedeon helped us care for sick children as well but with a sense of anger that he was forced to acknowledge the terrible circumstances that created so much illness inside the orphanage walls.

As children became ill, gripped by fever, with warm skin, redness over the chest and stomach that spread to arms and legs, a constant cough, headaches, and over time, chills and inability to eat, we would attend to them. Many of the afflicted died, especially after losing interest in drinking water. To me their suffering was unfathomable, and even at my incredibly young age of eleven, I asked for the reason that this curse had entered our home. Neil suggested perhaps that it was God's will, that evil had accompanied some of the street children, or that our chores and prayers had been done improperly.

While Gedeon also was helpful in caring for the children during their varied illnesses, he had no interest in science. To him the point of interest was not the cause of the malady but always the unfairness of an orphanage where children did not have the same opportunities as others, where parents could drop off their children forever, where resources were wasted on battles as compared to childcare. To Gedeon, life was about creating a better society.

As for me, I had a passion for asking why and finding solutions. I found an explanation for the children's illness on the day that I began to bathe and comfort those children who were particularly hot to the touch. Removing their clothing, I found what I believed to be the true nature of their malady. In fact, there appeared in the clothing and on the skin of these afflicted children tiny monsters of such a bizarre nature that they would bring goose bumps to whoever encountered them. And the smell, often so bad, of the children's skin wounds, I would not and could not forget.

Neil and I carefully inspected these creatures. The little gray monsters were barely visible, with pointed heads, six legs, and two projections from the tiny head. It appeared to me that those children who were ill often had such creatures in their clothes and on their skin. Those who shared the same bed seemed to also share the creatures and became sick together. Children too loud or wild to sleep in the common room seemed to be spared from the illness.

More importantly, some children had small areas of bleeding just where they had carried these tiny forms, as if they had been bitten by them. The more bleeding spots, the more certain the illness. And so I wondered what terrible particles these devils were injecting into the blood of the children. I carefully washed the children's bites with water to keep them clean and prevent the illness. And I thought, if I dared, I might let myself get bitten and see if in fact I too would get the very same illness. A bold idea to prove a point! Then when spring arrived and the orphanage's conditions improved, with less crowding, the tiny crawling beasts disappeared, and the sickness was gone. I found that caring for ill children gave me a feeling of invincibility.

Later that year, in springtime, another illness spread among all of us. It started with a runny nose, sore throat, and red eyes, and then predictably, a rash started below the scalp and spread first to the face and chest, then to the arms and legs. A few of the children developed breathing problems, and one of them died. All of us came down with this red-face disease except those who were living in a separate housing facility, usually because of their behavioral problems. We called them the rascal group. What would remain memorable to me was that several months later, when the rascal group rejoined the rest of us, the red-face disease came back to affect just them, as if someone had kept a record of who was yet to get this problem. Not one of us got the same sickness again, only those who had been spared the first time. For many years, I was left wondering why we all had seemed to be protected from a second round of this disease.

In March 1859, my headmaster informed me that two professors, also physicians, had made an appointment to meet with me. Because I had no known family and no identity other than what I had cultivated for myself in my school, such a meeting was a surprise and mystery to me. I had heard of benefactors who had chosen children of potential to support, and of course on occasion there were inquiries about adoption and fostering. We children had had experiences of speaking with clergy, teachers, donors, community volunteers, and city officials. But having my own personal visitors was a unique event.

In the office of our headmaster, which also served as the school's library, I was introduced to my guests.

"Jacob," said the headmaster, "Professors Ferdinand von Hebra and Ignaz Semmelweis have asked to speak with you. Jacob, these men were friends of your mother, and they are well-known physicians."

Now, up to this time, extraordinarily little had been said about my mother. Whether one was an orphan because one's parents were dead or because one simply had been abandoned mattered not at all to the children at my school. Two physicians coming here, where we were all no one, to see me specifically made my heart pound as it rarely did, and my mind jumped quickly to what I might have done.

"Jacob," began the younger, more dapper, more articulate Hebra, "we have come as a promise to your mother, a promise from twelve years ago that we, at the right time, would tell you about her distinguished life, about her death, and about her legacy and how she would like to be known to you."

"But if you are indeed friends with my mother, why now and not years ago—perhaps when I would have yearned for some identity?"

Hebra nodded and smiled. "Today we fulfill your mother's request as she made it to us under exceedingly difficult circumstances. She was never a colleague to argue or debate with."

Hebra continued, "Your mother was a physician and a scientist and a woman of great dignity, principle, and compassion. She had no family and grew up under the same conditions as you. She fought to become the first woman physician in Vienna, arguing for the importance of a woman doctor to treat women patients."

Then spoke the older man, Semmelweis. He seemed extremely uncomfortable and anxious, with large, sad eyes and a gray mustache. He looked downward at the floor and never at me. "Your mother died shortly after giving birth to you, of a malady called childbed fever. She was the first to recognize that women were dying needlessly because doctors, doctors like us, were not washing their hands and were spreading particles of death during deliveries. Ironically, she was a victim of the same malady."

I had never seen such sadness in the eyes of adults. I thought they might begin to cry at any moment, like a child who had fallen off his bicycle.

Both men paused, perhaps wondering how much of this a twelve-year-old could comprehend. And while I was not certain exactly how babies were produced or delivered, I had studied the spread of fevers and disease as extensively as I could.

Semmelweis continued, "At your mother's insistence, we brought to the medical attention of the medical community the cause of childbed fever, contaminated hands, as well as the method of its prevention: compulsory hand washing. Unfortunately, we have been neither understood nor believed. She would be disappointed in us; she would have never given up this fight."

Hebra was becoming impatient. He had completed his mission and was ready to excuse himself, feeling that more than enough had been said. "It is an intellectual battle that is not mine. Childbed fever is not my area of interest, and I have moved on to less controversial study matters. I carry with me every day the tragedy of your mother's death." Hebra extended his hand to me, and then he was gone.

Semmelweis put his head in his hands and continued to speak in a subdued and pathetic manner. His eyelids twitched. He apologized for letting my mother down and for losing the intellectual battle she'd been a part of. He was no longer the physician or scientist that he had been twelve years earlier. In fact, he believed that he was losing his mind and soul. And he informed me, apologetically, that his defense of the childbed fever work was over. So many considered him mentally unstable that he had begun to believe they might be correct.

I thought that these men must have really loved my mother to want to have this conversation with a twelve-year-old orphan.

Of the many, many questions to ask, I picked the two most important to me. First, I had a great curiosity about the childbed fever described and asked about the nature of these toxic particles that were causing the death of women. I also told Semmelweis about my experiences with the winter death and the red-face disease.

"Your winter death was typhus," he stated. "It is spread by lice and other tiny insects and occurs under crowded conditions such as in prisons and the military. Your red-face disease was measles, common in children and easily spread from one child to another."

"And what are these toxic particles that cause childbed fever and caused the death of my schoolmates?"

"That we do not know. There is no way to know. Your mother went as far as to mention on her deathbed that the animalcules of Leeuwenhoek might be causing death and disease, an idea considered most preposterous."

"Well, I am just a boy, and what I know, I have learned on my own. But my mind is slow to reject what my mother might have said on her deathbed." I moved on to my other, less complicated question. "Herr Semmelweis, who was my father?"

"Your mother believed that to you, he was of no importance."

"But you knew him?"

"Only in passing."

"And he is dead?"

"No, I cannot say he is dead."

"Then I must know more about him."

"Jacob, that is not part of the mission that your mother entrusted to me."

"But it is what I ask of you in the name of my mother and all that you owe her."

"Jacob, if he is alive, he is far, far away from Vienna."

And then I surprised myself, more influenced by my years of nonidentity than I would have thought. "Herr Semmelweis, if he is on earth, I will find him."

"Jacob, I will summon you next week. I have some contacts. I will find out if he is still living."

And that night my life was given purpose.

THE VIENNA MEDICAL SCHOOL

Herr Semmelweis asked to meet me at the Vienna Medical School, across the street from the orphanage, in the large conference room on the first floor. I had never been inside the familiar building, but I knew from my friends some of what went on there. It was easy to gain entrance through the back door, as the orphans were frequently summoned here. Those with abnormalities or deformities were particularly popular. They were poked and prodded, asked questions, and photographed. On occasion some type of operation would be performed on them, such as a fix for an abnormal mouth or lip. If you had a problem on your skin, they would cut if off and put it in a jar for everyone to look at. I had been told that if a child had a breathing problem, the professors would sound out his chest with their fingers as if they were beating on a drum, and the students would ooh and ah over the sounds that would so emanate. If you had a heart problem, they might all listen to your chest with a flexible tube. The doctors were said to be of all ages, some seeming barely older than we were. They argued, preached to each other, and took lots of notes.

In the basement there was sometimes a stretcher carrying a dead body. The doctors would shuttle between examining such bodies in the school and working in the adjacent hospital.

I found the large theater that was the meeting room. It had multiple levels with many benches laid out in a circle. There was a man addressing the full room. Older men in black suits, some with silly top hats, filled the front rows, and the higher the row, the younger were the doctors. With there being so many of them, I wondered why no one had been able to save my mother. I thought that with such an interest in shared wisdom, they would know everything. I also noticed there were just a few women, and they were mostly young—my mother would have been the oldest of them all. The seats were arranged like a horseshoe, with the speaker in the middle.

I listened to those in the back rows as the speaker finished his speech. One said that this was a wonderful opportunity for them to hear a well-known young surgeon from Edinburgh, who just happened to be here because he was honeymooning in Vienna. The speaker spoke of the great tragedy of death from wounds that did not heal, wounds that smelled badly. He was frustrated that the results of his surgical skills were being ruined after the operation was over. Much of what he said, I was able to understand.

He had intelligence and style, and he concluded his speech by imploring the others to help find answers. They applauded loudly in a way that I had not heard before, and some stood. I saw the respect they had for this individual in their faces, their posture. What he had said had led to loud conversation among the group. He had motivated these doctors to speak to each other. Even as a twelve-year-old with little education, I felt his passion.

As the meeting ended, I descended the stairs to get to Semmelweis, who was seated in the front row. The speaker approached Semmelweis just before I arrived. As they spoke, the guest hung on every word of the older man, as if he were the only person in the whole world who mattered. It was odd that the visitor seemed to treat Semmelweis with more deference and attention than the others who surrounded them.

"Ignaz," said the guest speaker, "as a physician and scientist I do not reject your childbed fever dogma, but it is problematic, controversial, and paradoxical—the hands of physicians as a cause of death and disease. But I have seen gangrenous tissue in my patients, the cause of which I do not understand."

Semmelweis just hung his head, not interested in further debate.

I saw the speaker's name on his white coat. He was Joseph Lister. He was only a decade older than I was, but I thought he was a great man or would become one. As they finished, I reintroduced myself to Herr Semmelweis.

But just before leaving, Lister interrupted and asked me who I was and why I was at the Vienna School of Medicine.

"I am an orphan," I said, "an orphan of no means. My mother died here. I am told she was killed after childbirth by doctors who did not wash their hands. I am in search of my father."

Lister crouched down. He shook my hand. He told me to always remember that such an injustice should never occur among the great doctors of the day. This stranger with his great vitality, piercing eyes, bushy beard and sideburns, and friendly manner walked toward his wife to leave. But then he turned to me and said, "When you become a doctor, perhaps you and your generation will do better. And yes, you must always wash your hands."

I so liked him and hoped I would see him again. Before him, no one had ever addressed me that way.

Semmelweis remained somber and defeated. He reminded me of some of our teachers who had given up on getting through to their students. As he followed Lister with his sad eyes, he muttered to himself, "A man who might have understood childbed fever."

Turning to me, Semmelweis said, "Your father is alive. His name is Luc Lavigne. He sells wine in Lille, France. He works at the Bigo winery. He is known to be a man of integrity. That is all that I know.

Son, I can do no more for you, as I can no longer even help myself. I am sorry that your presence so pains me. So this is my goodbye."

Courage might come from having nothing to lose. I knew then that I would find Lille, France, my father, and my destiny.

LEAVING
THE VIENNA
FOUNDLINGS

My initial plan was to leave the Vienna Foundlings by night and follow the Danube River through Austria to Germany. After reaching the Black Forest in Germany, I would find some steam engine to Lille in France. There, I would search the vineyards for the Bigo winery and find my father. Leaving the orphanage would not be a problem; many children got lost each week here, no one really cared, and at my age I was close to being put out into the world anyway.

I researched my plan with Neil and Gedeon. I hoped that Neil would leave with me. It was a special and tense night—three orphans around a table in the library, a place of relative quiet and safety for us for years. We had met there many times before to discuss our role in the orphanage and the greater world, a world that none of us really understood. We had met to discuss ways to deal with teachers and to help the younger children and to guess what our eventual escape to the outside would be. Of course, there also were times when we were treated poorly, made to feel worthless—those were the times we would comfort each other.

That night we studied maps, the fauna and flora of the Danube, distances, and walking time. Gedeon also was helpful in describing the political state of the Habsburg empire and the current state of Europe. He was ready to leave the orphanage and explore the world, but his world was different from mine, and his journey was yet to be defined.

"Gedeon, you can join us. There is nothing here for you. I am searching for my father but also for my purpose."

"Jacob," Gedeon replied, "there are many dangers outside in addition to the disease and death here. I admire you for your courage to find a better life. And I will make my journey as well. But I am neither ready nor sure what path I will take. But I will make my mark, and it will be my own."

I spread out some maps of Austria and its surrounding neighbor countries. "Neil," I said, "the distance between Vienna and Lillie is about seven hundred miles. At least four hundred miles can be negotiated by following the river itself through the Austrian towns of Durnstein, Melk, and Linz. The river will empty at the site of Munich, Germany, and the Black Forest. From there it will be several hundred miles more to Lille."

"Jacob, we are in excellent physical condition. I once measured our walk around the Foundlings at three miles per hour. We could be in Lille, walking at eight hours per day, in about twenty days. If we found a German steam engine to take us to Lille from Germany, it would be sooner. There is also the possibility of acquiring bicycles or having fishing boats ease the arduousness of the trip."

Gedeon said, "Well, you might look odd at age twelve strutting along the Danube or riding in a steam engine."

"And some of the soldiers, Gedeon—how old are they?" I asked.

"I have heard that some are not much older than you are."

"And how old do I look?"

"Jacob, you have started filling out some. Our constant chores have put some muscle on all of us. You do not have a beard yet, but you have the making of a mustache. And your good looks— those blue eyes and jet-black hair—will help you make friends easily."

"Jacob," said Neil, "it is not about how old we look. We have been independent for as long as we can remember. We have been resourceful. And you have always made wise decisions and shown good judgment. No one should doubt that we can make this trip."

Both Neil and I filled two large sacks with food we'd saved and leftovers we'd found in the kitchen, mostly breads, beans, cheese, and some smoked meats. We always had plenty of simple surplus clothing, donated secondhand but very adequate, especially with winter having passed. We were also confident we could find some berries, grapes, and apple trees along the way. We would drink the water from the river. There would be some dangers. Countries were at war, and soldiers were everywhere. There were also wolves and brown bears. We would be unarmed. But it was springtime, and we did not expect challenges from the weather.

This journey would require resilience, but we were already steeled by the Vienna Foundlings—its gift to those who survived the place.

At dusk on the night we were to leave, Neil approached me with a somber and embarrassed look. His usually sad eyes looked even sadder, a single tear running down his cheek before he even began to speak.

"I cannot go. I am overtaken with fear and doubts. We have many of the same life experiences, but we are not the same. Jacob, you are full of life, optimism, curiosity, and hope. You challenge life every day; you believe in better times. You are strong, the smartest person any of us has ever known, always asking why things must be as they are. Neither I nor your teachers believe that you are only twelve years old. You never belonged here with us. You are likely descended from some seed of greatness. I am not like you. I am not your partner in changing our inevitable dark fate and certainly not in changing the world. I have already died here. The abuses we both know that have been too cruel to describe—the isolation, the disease and death that we have seen in our friends—they have left me without energy, without the life force necessary for the incredible journey that you are planning. And when you do find your father, of whatever temperament he may be, I will still be the orphan whose parents left me here alone. No, Jacob, I will spend the rest of my empty life right here. Your chances for success, whatever they are, will be better without me."

"Neil, whatever the tragedy of our lives has been so far, there is always hope. King Arthur, Beowulf, Odysseus … you know them as I do. People find their courage when they are challenged. Our experiences give us resilience and offer us hope."

But Neil could only smile and shake his head. "I will surely miss you, Jacob. I will remember you as the person that I could not be."

"You will not die here, Neil. We both will rise above our misfortune."

And so I would face my journey alone, without my only loyal friend in the world. And while I was unsure of where this journey would lead, Neil was right. I wanted life to be better, not just for me but for all who suffered.

DEATH OF PAUL

As I approached the Bigo winery, I had a new perspective on the innate kindness of people and the gift of natural beauty in everyday life. Despite a life of poverty, abuse, confinement, and depravation, my life had changed. My religious teachings had taken on new meaning with my introduction to the physical world that was part of my journey. The Danube River cut through green mountains, surrounded by birds and flowers of all colors. I was able to study the hundreds of bird species, so large and so small, and their diverse ways of bonding together, including geese who flew in their V-shaped formation with the leaders in front, easing the way for the others. On some days, the water was so clear that I could see in it the reflections of giant pine trees and the sky itself. I sailed the river with a fisherman who assisted me in my journey with few questions asked. Soldiers shared a meal with me around a campfire. I cautiously passed through cities—Durnstein with its seven-hundred-year-old castle, the castle where King Richard had been held captive by the duke of Austria; Melk with its abbey monastery and stone houses, all with large oval windows, pointed towers, and flying buttresses; and Linz with its goats and grasslands that introduced me to what I would see in the vineyards of Lille.

But what I would remember most about my journey was Paul. I met him on a night when I was sleeping under the stars, but close to an abandoned barn. I heard a person moaning, whimpering. It was outside Durnstein, and I had been walking for several weeks. I entered the barn in the light of dusk to see a middle-aged man in the worst condition possible, thin and dirty despite the opportunities of the river. His chest was bare, his trousers mud-caked, and at the right leg his trousers had been ripped from the leg itself. He smelled like death, like some of the children whom I had seen die from the creatures or what Semmelweis had called the typhus.

When he saw me, he cried out for help. "I need some water. I am in tough shape."

"Yes, I can bring you some water from the river." The barn was close enough to the river for us to hear its roar and hope for its healing nature.

I proceeded to bring him water. He was barely able to drink, but he drank some of the water and poured the rest on his face.

"And food?" I asked.

"I am very sick, too sick to eat."

"Why are you here?" I asked.

"I have no reason to lie," he said. "I am a fugitive from prison. But my escape was only partially successful. You can see my leg. The shackles have broken into the skin. The leg has hurt me more each day, and with the fever and chills and aches, I could no longer continue."

His bare leg had a fiery redness that went from his ankle where the shackles had cut through his leg all the way up to his groin. A whitish substance was pouring out from the wound at the ankle and was the source of the horrendous smell. I could see the bone at the bottom of the wound.

I spent several days trying to help him. In fact, I had committed to myself that I would stay by his side. I poured water on his wound and on his whole body, for he was very warm to the touch. He was always dizzy and could not even sit up. His breathing was rapid, as if he could not get enough air.

He told me that his name was Paul. He had been a successful farmer, and somewhere in Austria he had a son and a wife, but he had long been separated from them as he had been in prison for years after killing a man while in a rage. He was very sad that his son would not grow up with a father. He complimented me on my feelings of compassion and efforts to understand what was wrong with him.

I told him that I too had grown up without a father and was not sure what difference it made.

As sick as he was, he wanted to speak with me. His words always came out slowly, and his mouth was dry. I think he feared that his death was imminent, and he had some things to say.

"You have a kindness about you, son. You learn in prison that no one is all good or all bad and that kindness often prevails. I made too many mistakes in life. There are so many things that I would do differently. Mostly, I let my family down, and I do not know if my son will grow up the right way without me. One thing I know is that all people are alike, no matter what they look like or where they come from. If I had the chance to do it all over again, I would become a doctor, or a poet or a priest. They see the true drama of life, and they can change people for the better. You could be a doctor, and a good one, one who would care for both the rich and the poor and always know the right thing to do."

"Yes, a famous man from Edinburgh whom I recently met also said I should become a doctor. And he wanted me to understand the cause of my mother's death. That is what I will try to do. But to just be a doctor, I do not know. They don't seem to know very much, and they killed my mother by having dirty hands."

"A farmer learns to attend to his fields over time," said Paul. "You compare one way of planting with another. After many years you know what's best for your farm, what works and what doesn't, when to plant, when to plow, and when to reap. There are so many ways a person's body can go wrong. Diseases are too complicated for a doctor to always know the right treatment for them, but they learn over time what's best for a person, just like the farmer learns what's best for his field."

"I guess I still need to learn who I am. I want to be like the heroes I have read about, more than just an orphan destined to be no one. There are things I am ignorant about, those things that you learn from a parent. But I have the courage of Ulysses. Sleeping on the shores of a river in the dark of night, joining the campfire of strangers, climbing an apricot tree—these are a few of the many things I am fearless about."

I wanted to help Paul as I had helped so many children in the orphanage. I washed his wound frequently in water, remembering that washing hands prevented childbed fever. But despite my giving him water over several days and trying to have him eat some of the bread that I still had left to share, he only got worse. The redness and heat of his leg spread past his groin to his stomach, as if the malady had a life of its own. Soon he was speaking incessantly, making little sense, and asking me for forgiveness as if I were his priest. He went from feeling very warm to having ice-cold feet. His breathing went from fast to slow. And on the fifth day of my tending to him, he took one long, slow breath and then stopped breathing altogether.

I was no stranger to death. I could only bury him thinly below grasses and leaves. I assumed that was the right thing to do.

That night I dreamed about this dead man who had seemed to see some good things in me. And I remembered the story of my mother's death and relived the deaths of the children who had died of the typhus. And I smelled that smell of death. I dreamed of animals too small to see. They were of all shapes and sizes. They moved quickly in circles, tumbling and clumping together. I saw these creatures on the hands of the doctors who had killed my mother. They had invaded Paul's leg wound and had been in the mouths of the insects that bit the children. Semmelweis was wrong. Childhood fever was not about poison. These were deadly, living creatures.

I thought of these tiny animals that would become my calling.

I had followed the Danube from Vienna to its mouth in the Black Forest. The path became more mountainous, and the trees, tall pines, seemed to grow so tightly together that they blocked the sun and made my compass a necessity for keeping my orientation. As I moved away from the river, it became more difficult to scavenge for food, ask for the charity of fishermen, or find apricots or apples. The bag of supplies that I'd brought from the orphanage kitchen also was dwindling. But deep into the woods, the smells of a campfire and the frying of fish, smells I had become familiar with, gave me some hope of satisfying my hunger and perhaps finding someone to speak with and get advice from about the last leg of my journey to France.

As I approached the campfire, a man who saw that I was just a boy shouted to me that I was welcome to join them, but that I might want to come toward them slowly and let them warn me about who they were.

As I approached them, I quickly understood the warning. The leader of the group, whom I could see by the light of the campfire, looked barely human. His head was large, and his forehead more prominent than any forehead I had ever seen. His skin was very tanned, and his black hair hung to his shoulders. As I came closer in the dwindling light, I could see that he had no eyebrows and that his nose was bent out of shape. Two other men had somewhat similar appearances—they were also dark and had long black hair and deformities. The lumps on their faces made them appear like some cobblestone streets in Vienna. One of the men had a normal appearance but resembled the others, as if related to them but spared the calamity that had affected the other three.

Because they seemed to be friendly, I cautiously moved forward to join them at the campfire, fearful but with the courage that had been fostered by my other encounters on my trip.

"My name is Basil," said the man who had called out to me. I noted that he walked with difficulty. He motioned me to sit by the fire.

One of the men reached for a frying pan, and I saw that he had a clawlike hand.

Basil introduced me to his friends and offered me some fish and bread on a wooden slab.

"My name is Jacob, and I am on a trip to see my father in France."

"Jacob, you are a brave soul, and I want you to know you have nothing to fear from us," said Basil.

The man with claws for hands also welcomed me. "My name is Laslo. We are all from Hungary and are making this trip along the river, having started out from Margaret Island. These are my other brothers, Andras and Naaman."

Naaman, the normal-appearing one, came forward to shake my hand.

"May I ask what has happened to them?"

"Have you heard about lepers, Jacob?"

"Yes, I have read the story in the Bible."

"We come from a leper colony. It is on an island near Vienna called Margaret, on the shores of the Danube. Just as in the biblical story, we are outcasts, considered unclean and persecuted wherever we go."

"But what happened to you to cause your misfortune? Why does Naaman look normal?"

"We are all brothers," said Laslo. "Our skin started becoming like this many years ago, as did our father's. He died in a very terrible condition. Naaman never became ill. He remains healthy despite constantly being around us. He has been able to guide us and support us with his work on the railroad."

"But why? Why did this happen to you?" I asked.

"We do not know. Some say it is the curse of God. But we have lived our lives in a very clean way, without sin. It is others who have sinned against us."

I joined the group around the campfire, my hunger much more intense than any feelings of revulsion for these friendly travelers.

"Jacob, how is a young boy like yourself walking along the Danube alone, and why would you not be terrified of us as the sun set and you saw our frightening appearances? Are you not afraid to catch whatever has afflicted us?"

"Well, I won't say that I am not upset by seeing your faces, especially up close. But I am generally not one to be fearful. I was told by one of the older boys in the orphanage that we were never taught fear because we never had parents who cared about us. And if you mean catching something like from an animalcule, I have learned not to fear them despite the fact that they killed my mother."

"Animalcules," said Laslo, the one with the clawlike hands. "What are animalcules?"

"I was told that on her deathbed my mother thought small animals, too small to see, might cause sickness."

"What illnesses?" asked Laslo.

"Childbed fever and perhaps some sickness that I saw among the children in the orphanage. May I ask where you are all headed?"

"Naaman has heard that in Germany, and even farther north in Scandinavia, there is a new spirit of science. We are seeking an explanation for our misfortune and perhaps even a treatment to make us well again. Jacob, you propose an animalcule, a new one on us, but we must consider even the strangest hypothesis. If Jesus could cure the leper, perhaps God can teach man to do the same."

"You believe that God could teach a man to cure a leper?" I asked. The idea caused me great excitement and overwhelmed my mind.

"Jacob, I think God can lead man to do many great things."

"I would like to believe that too," I said, "and I would surely want to be one of those whose hand God guides. I am interested in those ideas. And what if an animalcule caused your sickness? Doesn't that sound more likely than it being a curse from God?"

The whole group laughed but also smiled at me with admiration.

"If that were true, could you not get sick from us?" asked Basil.

"Well," I said, "Naaman remains well, and he has traveled with you. It may be my mistake in life, perhaps my Achilles heel, but I will not fear the animalcules."

Again, there was amusement, and like many others in the past, they did not know what to think of me.

"Perhaps you would like to come with us to Germany or Norway and visit the universities there," said Naaman.

"No, I must head toward France, to Lille, to find my father."

"And how will you get to Lille?" Naaman asked.

"I am not sure. Hopefully by railroad or carriage, but if necessary, I will walk there."

Then Naaman stepped forward and hugged me like a father might hug a child. "Jacob, I am a man familiar with the steam engines. There is indeed a railroad to Paris that will get you very close to Lille. I will take you there. It is a two-day journey. I can make it happen. My brothers will wait here for my return."

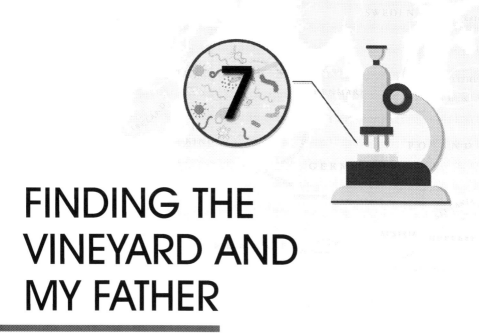

FINDING THE VINEYARD AND MY FATHER

My moment had come, as I had found the vineyards of Lille and in particular the Bigo vineyard. I had followed the river, slept on its banks, and accepted the kindness of many strangers. I had listened to their directions and accepted their gifts of food, a compass, and a warm jacket. I'd fought hunger on occasion, as well as fear of the dark and of howls that I did not understand. I had sat naked as I washed my clothes and waited for them to dry in the sun. I had seen the great beauty of nature and the harsh realities of death from disease. I had been guided to a railroad by the brother of lepers. I never had been tempted to turn back to the relative safety of my orphanage home. I was now in a lush valley surrounded by green hills and growing vines and trees. Those whom I'd found on the surrounding mountain trails all knew the Bigo vineyard.

As I approached the vineyard, there was a sweet smell, a cool wind, and only the sound of the rustling of trees. I met a young boy, friendly, who introduced himself as Pierre and who was tall like me, with blue eyes, black hair, and an olive complexion. He was perhaps a year or two younger than I was. He looked more like me than most in the orphanage had. He approached me with great curiosity.

I had kept my clothes clean, and my health was still good; in fact, I was quite fit from the miles I had walked. But I feared that my baggy trousers and simple white frock were too obviously out of place here. Also, the fact that I was a twelve-year-old, traveling alone, added to my apprehension.

"Are you here to see the winery?" the boy asked.

"I am."

"We have a very warm sun here and cool winds. Nice soil. This was always the best place for wine making. Still the best place for growing grapes. But times are bad. My dad is so sad, crying about his wine."

"I have been told that a Luc works here."

"He does. That's my dad. Are you wanting to see him?"

"I have traveled for weeks to find him, to ask him questions about myself. I am from Vienna."

"You want to work here?"

"I do not. I know nothing about wines."

"Then you know my father from a trip of his to Vienna?"

"No, I have never met him."

"I don't mean to be rude," said Pierre, "but we don't have a lot of strangers walk in here, certainly not kids."

"Yes, I suppose I am not your usual visitor."

"I can't help but notice that like me, you have really black hair, blue eyes, and wide shoulders," he told me. "Are you good at fishing, swimming, and hiking, he asked? These are my favorite activities."

"No," I answered.

"Then I guess we are not really that alike.

"I am good at taking care of children, reading books, and traveling seven hundred miles to find Luc."

Pierre had had enough of our conversation and reluctantly allowed me in. "Luc runs this vineyard and did so with success until recently. You can find him in the warehouse ahead."

"Success until recently?" I asked.

"Yes, the wine has spoiled, and a vineyard without wine is the end of work for all of us. Most workers have been sent home. The spoiled wines have changed my father and others whose entire lives revolve around the vineyards. The great vineyards of France are right here, but there is a curse afflicting them that no one understands."

Pierre continued, "You seem out of place here. But my father is a kind man. And if you have traveled weeks to see him, as you say, I know he will meet with you and be nice to you."

As we walked together to the warehouse, I could not keep myself from asking Pierre about his family.

"Your father is a good man, I have heard."

"Yes, of course. He is like a father to everyone. But he likes to travel—leaves me home. He's always searching for something more to his life. He is known for his successful vineyard, but somehow that has never been enough for him."

"And you have brothers or sisters?"

"Not here in Lille. I am an only child. I have been told that my father, who travels the world with his wines, might have been married before he met my mother, many times before—that he has had wives in London, Paris, and Vienna. My mother left him years ago. So he tells me always to find the right woman and stay with her."

We arrived at the warehouse.

The warehouse doors opened, showing vast, empty, poorly lit spaces and a few desks. It was an incredibly quiet place and looked like it had been abandoned. The desk chairs were unoccupied but for one man, sitting quite alone.

Pierre introduced me to the large, dark, broad-shouldered man. He had the same blue eyes as mine, the same as Pierre's. He smelled of wine. His white tunic was stained purple like a world map. He sat behind briefcases, papers, and empty wine bottles. He appeared sad but kind and welcoming.

I, who had always had a profound sense of equanimity, felt at this moment the rapid heartbeat and dry mouth that were so often described in the novels I had read. And for a moment, I asked myself why I was there. Looking for identity? But identity had never truly mattered to me. To ask about my mother? But the Vienna physicians knew more about my mother than this man likely did. To ask for his apology? For what gain? No, I was there to capture a sense of my identity and then to move on to somewhere else.

"I am Jacob from Vienna."

He stood up. His eyes locked on mine. He flinched in pain, as if he had just received bad news. I was sure he knew who I was.

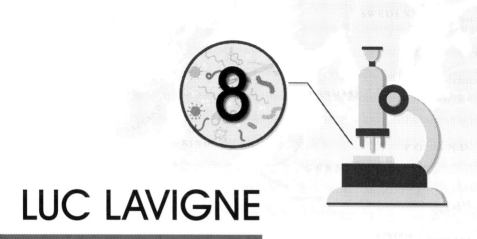

LUC LAVIGNE

M aybe it was because I had spoken to so few people on my
journey or because so few people had listened to me in my
life. Or perhaps it was because I had never felt so safe as
now, resting in his family home, or maybe in fact because he was
my father—but I could not stop talking throughout the night and
listening to someone who was sharing a different world experience
with me.

I certainly did not know the proper way to speak to a father who
had abandoned me at birth. "How do you leave a wife who is going
to have a child?" I asked with curiosity and no malice. "Even I know
about the marital vows that people take."

"Truly, I was not a good husband, and I have many regrets—now,
today, more than ever. Your mother was such a fine person, a perfect
person, a brilliant person who cared so much for her patients. As a
woman doctor, she was sensitive to the poor treatment, the unequal
treatment, that women received. She was intensely dedicated to
changing that inequity and to inspiring more woman to join the field.
The problem is that your mother was never married to me. She was
married to medicine and could not seem to be married to both of us."

"Can't you be married and still be dedicated to your work?" I asked.

"Even when we were on holiday, her thoughts were with her work, her obsession with what she would call the secret of childbed fever. On occasion, when I would tell her about my back pain or my sore throat, she would look at me with surprise and tell me that she had seen true suffering."

"Well, she saw women dying, I have been told."

"I just could not be important in her world. She was a saint, a genius by birth, a doctor as Hippocrates described. I was a wine merchant with no commitment to mankind. I was selling wine in Vienna when we met at a fundraiser for the hospital. I never thought to apologize for who I was or for how insignificant my work might be. Eventually, I left to come back to the beauty of my life here in Lille. I knew she would be better off and perhaps not even notice I was gone."

"But did you know that she was pregnant when you left her?"

"I did, but I could not be a father under those conditions. It is now, seeing you, that I realize what I did was wrong."

"Did you know that I existed at all?"

"I was told that she had died of childbed fever while giving birth. I had assumed that this malady, whatever it was, took the life of the child as well, or that if the child survived, it would be in a condition even worse than death."

"So you really didn't care if I'd lived or died?"

"Jacob, for a twelve-year-old boy, you don't mince words. I am prepared and able to make it up to you. Stay with us. It is only me and Pierre. I can provide for you. You can learn the trade if our business survives, live in one of the most beautiful places in the world, go to the university and catch up on your studies. Is that why you have come to find me here? For financial support?"

"I came here across the lands to find out who I was, who I was supposed to be. I believed that meeting my father would help chart my course. But yes, it is true that I really have no place to go."

My father had offered me some type of support, and that was more than I had ever had before. I thought of how the children in my orphanage would trade places with me now. I did not want to insult this honest man, but I didn't want to be a wine merchant, and I wondered if I was more like my mother, whom I'd never met, than I was like my father.

"I am so very tired that I will accept your offer. And I have nowhere else to go and no one who cares a whit about me. I appreciate your kindness. I would like to stay here with you temporarily as I try to understand my life and what you have told me. But I know already that a beautiful life in these vineyards is not my destiny."

"Jacob, you have come here at a most crucial time in my life. In fact, our very livelihood, the wine industry, is in jeopardy. Perhaps my crisis and your shocking arrival were meant to come together in time. Sometimes in life we end up where we need to be."

As I knew little about the subject of fate, I asked simply, "Can the grapes no longer grow?"

"No," he said with a smile. "It is more complicated than that. Our distillery is one of the finest in France, and it has been in my family— well, your family too—for generations. But now when our grapes are fermented, they do not produce wine but only a rotten liquid, a ghastly concoction that smells of death. This bad fermentation will bankrupt us eventually."

"And how may I help with this?"

"You cannot, but I will tell you about a man who can perhaps save us. There is a new dean at the Lille university. They say that as a rule such deans are very smart, but this individual is beyond that. He is a chemist who has just discovered something new about chemical structure—how substances reflect light and how they are shaped. He sees things that are too small for others to see. Most importantly, he is here to help the community, to use science to help the industries and factories in Lille. It is a new concept—a community-based university using science to help people."

"Sir, I am excited to hear about this man, for what you describe as science is, I believe, tied up with my own passion and fate."

"You will meet him tomorrow. He comes to sample our wine, our slime."

"His name?" I asked.

"Pasteur, Louis Pasteur."

LOUIS PASTEUR
AND FATE

The staff of the winery had anticipated the visit of Dean Louis Pasteur. He arrived by horse and carriage, an elegant-looking carriage with a well-dressed driver and two muscular, well-behaved black horses. I sensed this might be a special moment in my life. Louis Pasteur bounced out of the carriage and took in the expanse and beauty of the vineyard. For what seemed like an eternity, he said nothing. Surely, even such a scientist must have appreciated the natural beauty of the vineyard. A group of a dozen employees, including Luc, Pierre, and me, waited for his instructions. One could feel the tension in the air. After all, the livelihood of all in attendance might depend on Louis Pasteur, a man of science but not a man of the vineyards or wine industry.

My first impression was that he was but an ordinary man, not much taller than I was. He had a large forehead and a short, snub nose. Mr. Pasteur looked to be in his thirties. He had a black, thick mustache and black beard that extended to his ears. His eyebrows pointed upward at their ends. He wore a black suit and vest with a white shirt buttoned to the neck. His dark eyes gave him an expression of thoughtfulness and wonder. He was not impolite but was not prepared to waste time. He was observant, eyes roving from one person to another and taking in the rolling green hills and large warehouses. The air carried the smell of horses and the musty smell of grapes. There was a light rain, and Pasteur had become a bit wet, but he could be drenched and still have a dignified look about him.

Luc made some introductions, including a quick reference to me as his son who had just traveled on his own from Vienna. Pasteur locked eyes with me but had more important things on his mind than exploring a comment about a boy who had been given an odd introduction. In a confident voice, he addressed the group.

"I am not an expert on wine," said Pasteur, "at least not at this point in my life. I am a scientist, and I try to solve problems in a logical way. Let me tell you the secret that leads me to success in what I do. It is tenacity, and I will be tenacious in studying your wine samples. Success favors only minds that are diligently looking and preparing to discover solutions. It will be a great learning experience for me. The more I study nature, the more I stand amazed at the work of the Creator. Please take me to your barrels and vats."

Luc brought him small bottles of good wine. Pasteur smelled and tasted the wine, admitting that his knowledge of wine was limited. He labeled several bottles of that wine and asked to see the barrels where the spoiled wine sat. He tasted and smelled that wine too but did not extend any comments or even make the face that others who were watching were making. They stared at him with amusement, as if bad wine should have provoked a more impressive reaction. Every sample was carefully labeled. His visit was surprisingly short.

"My work here today is ended. I will return to my laboratory. I will be back each day. Please be ready to provide me with additional samples."

I wanted to know this man, Pasteur. I wanted to know what he would do with the wine samples and what his thought process was regarding problem-solving, and of course, I wanted to tell him about my life experiences, my ideas, and the stories about childbed fever from Vienna. But I bided my time. I hoped that I might someday speak with him when he was less intense and preoccupied. The problem of childbed fever also could be resolved in a logical way.

In the meantime, the course of my life had changed. I had a place to live and even a bedroom that I could call my own. I had clothes that Pierre had given me—his clothes, which fit well. The three of us, Luc, Pierre, and I, ate our meals together.

"Luc, or if I may call you Father, I have grown up with nothing. I had no name, no family, no possessions to call my own. I saw abuse of children far too ugly to describe. I saw death, disease, and hopelessness. But I never lost faith. I had teachers; I learned to read. I was inspired by many heroes in books. I had a friend, and I had a desire to understand the world around me. When Herr Semmelweis visited me and told me about my mother, I had a new hero and a new reason for living. And now, your kindness and your clothes and shelter have only sparked my search for what my role in this life should be."

"Jacob, I can already see that you will be a good man. You have the wisdom of your mother and, well, good looks—the blue eyes, the broad frame—like me."

Over several days, I had many discussions with my half brother, and I learned from him about normal life. He was not an orphan, and he seemed to have been given a life of ease. He taught me about fishing, hunting, and cooking, and although he was a bit younger than I was, he knew about drinking all types of wine. He seemed kind and very much interested in taking me along on his next fishing trip. It might have been owing to my lack of life experience or the serious nature I'd needed to develop to survive in the orphanage, but the life he described, although quite wonderful, was just not right for me.

I explored the vineyards and helped with the picking of grapes as the staff awaited answers to the blight. I appreciated everything around me—the sun, the wind, the frequent rain, the new foods and tastes, the feel of soil. While now I realized the overwhelming deprivation that had been my life, I was nevertheless more interested in what I was calling science in learning about life itself than I was in enjoying those simple pleasures that I had been introduced to. This man, Louis Pasteur—I believed he might be seeing life in an analogous way to how I saw it.

We saw Pasteur and his assistants come and go, collecting samples but not giving any reports of progress. I was interested in Pasteur's every move, but for a brief moment my mind was distracted by one his assistants, the most beautiful woman I had ever seen. She looked at me for a brief moment too, but for two seconds, not one. But it was Pasteur with whom I fervently wished to speak.

After several months, it was my day to speak with him. I waited as he exited his carriage. He had arrived alone. I boldly asked for his attention and told him succinctly that my mother had died of childbed fever, and I was seeking answers to that malady. He listened and responded. He no longer seemed hurried.

"When I see a young person like you, it inspires in me two sentiments—tenderness for who you are and respect for who you might become. What you know about Vienna, a wonderful place of science, is music to me. Science knows no country because knowledge belongs to humanity. It is the torch that illuminates the world. One does not ask of one who suffers, 'What is your country?' I learned about science at an early age, your age, and I do not take your enthusiasm lightly. I am sorry that your mother died at childbirth. It is a problem that we hear about occasionally in France. Of course, I am not a physician and am not trained in disease and cures. We do know that patients sometimes die in hospitals from fever that develops in the hospital itself. I invite you to return to my laboratory with me, and we can discuss your experiences. In addition, I will show you what we have learned so far about the spoiled wine. And perhaps you may want to pack some clothes. You may choose to stay in the laboratory for a day or more."

I remembered our Greek mythology book—the Fates, the three goddesses who assigned destinies to mortals. Even Zeus was unable to recall their decisions.

THE PASTEUR
LABORATORY

It was my first time in a horse and carriage, although many had passed me on my journey to Lille. I found myself not inhibited at all while sitting next to the dean of the Lille University, bouncing as I tried to speak intelligently but only feeling a sense of anticipation and excitement. I continued to describe my experiences with disease and death. I suspected that this man was not sure what to make of me, but he did listen intently. Of particular interest to him was my assertion that my own mother had died of childbed fever caused by animalcules of some kind on the hands of the doctors attending to her.

"Your father has told me about you. Raised in an orphanage, you came from Vienna to Lille on your own to find him," he stated with some incredulity.

"That is true. I walked much of the way. I came to find my destiny."

"Meaning what?" asked Pasteur.

"I was not destined to die in my orphanage. I could have easily done so from typhus. My mother died of childbed fever, but she was a doctor and a scientist. She discovered the cause of childbed fever, but her work was not done. And I learned of this from Herr Semmelweis, also a doctor and a scientist. Surely, you must know him?"

"I do not, but I am not a physician, and my work is not with patients or with pregnant women."

"I have also met Dr. Joseph Lister, a man who also believes in washing one's hands."

"Joseph Lister of Edinburgh? You know him as well?" Now Pasteur was smiling, as if I was indeed an amusement. "I do know of Lister and his work on understanding wounds. He has visited and spoken in Paris. Who else do you know?"

"I know Paul, a man who escaped from prison and then died because of a wound on his leg. I cared for him much like a doctor would have, and he complimented me on my compassionate attitude. I would like to know why he died as I attended to him."

"Well, son, we can put your experiences and curiosity to work. I look for answers to important questions, and you seem to want to do the same."

We arrived at the laboratory in just an hour.

Mr. Pasteur's assistants greeted us. There was Andre, who was older than Mr. Pasteur and who appeared kindly, with a white beard and rotund, rosy cheeks, a bit like Saint Nick but not as friendly. He gave commands to the others. Marie Laurent had a pretty face and dark hair parted at the center of her scalp. And yes, there was Adrienne, a student some years older than I. She reminded me of Aphrodite from the mythology books I'd read, but her hair was orange.

Pasteur led the way, and I was soon in a large room, the laboratory, with light reflected through large open windows. The room smelled like rubbing alcohol and contained numerous wooden desks and several wooden tables. There were shelves all over the laboratory walls. Most striking of all were the glass flasks, large and small, some with round bottoms, some tall and thin, some like large jars with wide mouths. Behind a desk, a colleague of Pasteur was looking—or rather, squinting—through a golden tube. It was bronze in color, with transparent glass on top, about a foot long, and there was a base below the tube and a mirror below the base. I saw beauty in that golden tube.

Pasteur and his assistant Andre both glanced through the instrument, which they called a microscope. Pasteur took some time between glances through the microscope to tell me that they had been looking at the wine samples during the normal wine fermentation process for weeks.

The group had studied the grapes-to-wine process by examining numerous samples of good wine. Pasteur summarized their findings as I tried to comprehend them.

"Having expected a simple chemical reaction, a reaction that turns two different substances into one, we have found instead— under the microscope—spherical dense globules circling around the field of vision, with bud-like projections developing around odd spherules and eventually breaking away from each other as if alive. What is important, Jacob, is that we have considered that these particles are alive and a necessary part of fermentation."

I was surprised that Pasteur was taking the time to explain his work to me.

"After weeks of study, we are now quite sure that wine fermentation requires living organisms and is not just a chemical reaction. Look through the microscope, son, and see the globules swimming around in the wine and producing their own."

I couldn't contain my excitement to view living things too small to see with one's own eye. "So there are living things that one can see only with this instrument?" I asked. "Perhaps they are dangerous, can cause death?"

"No," Pasteur laughed. "This is the fermented wine that we drink! These living globules are safe and friendly."

But he saw my enthusiasm, my passion to try to understand these things of nature. And he was bothered by my question. "Jacob, your interest in our work is quite amazing. Your enthusiasm is extraordinary for a boy of your age. I told Luc that I would offer you a place to stay here with my lab workers and scientists. There are quarters adjacent to the laboratory and a kitchen as well. There is a library where you can study. You can prepare specimens and work here for as long as you like. Perhaps we can get you back to the vineyards on weekends. What do you think about my offer?"

"Sir, having a place to stay with my father in the vineyards was my good fortune. However, this chance to be in a laboratory with a scientist is not simply good fortune but the start of my pathway to a life of meaning and an opportunity to fulfill my destiny. Mr. Pasteur, this will be my great honor, my turn of fortune. I believe that my mother would want me to be right here with you."

"Then tomorrow we will begin to understand the problem of spoiled wine."

Andre, who had been silent, wondering how a twelve-year-old boy could start to work for a renowned scientist without papers or formal education, now joined the conversation. "And Mr. Pasteur, in addition to the spoiled wine, we have been asked to look at some spoiled milk as well."

"We will begin to look at both the spoiled samples tomorrow. Let's start early in the morning."

Marie Laurent took me aside to tell me that she would show me to my quarters, where students and assistants lived and worked.

"I think you may be with us for a while," she said. "You will find our accommodations simple but comfortable. We will ask your father to send some more of your clothes here in the morning. The lab assistants and other help share a kitchen next to the laboratory. You can prepare your meals there. It is quite safe to work around the facility and even explore the dense wooded area. And we have a library with books from the University of Lille. There are some manuals about physics and the principles of microscopy."

"Thank you, Marie Laurent. I am overwhelmed by the kindness I have found here."

My first night in the University of Lille laboratory and its adjacent quarters felt comfortable. Later in the evening, there was a knock on the door of my dormitory-like room.

As I opened the door, Adrienne, the Aphrodite-like laboratory assistant, gave me a forced smile. "I came to chat with you, Jacob, assuming you have a moment."

Of course, I invited her in with excitement and apprehension. I had little experience with teenage girls like Adrienne.

The room was small, but there was a bed and a desk. It was dusk, and there was still light coming in from the window as she sat down at the desk chair, looking beautiful in a white laboratory coat that accented her long red hair. She seemed much more comfortable than I.

"Jacob, the twelve-year-old orphan who made his way to Lille by following the Danube—and who Louis suspects may be some type of savant."

"Savant? Meaning?"

"It is a French word for genius or a person of great intellectual ability, perhaps at the expense of everyday social skills." She could not stop herself from a brief laugh.

"As an orphan, I was taught to read by some very good teachers and guided by some older friends. I tried to read about science but also about the great heroes of Greek mythology and biblical stories."

"That would hardly make you a genius."

"But also, I had a mother, whom I never met, who was a doctor who delivered babies and made a great scientific discovery. Maybe I have some of her traits. I have heard that she was admired by everyone, and I suspect that one wine merchant and several doctors were likely in love with her. Why does everyone have to tie me to my orphanage? Each of us who grew up there was different from the others."

"Jacob, I suspect you will always be the boy from the orphanage."

"And I assume that you must have grown up in a better place, with lots of family members?"

"Well, we are talking about you, not me. And I am wise enough to keep my own upbringing separate from my work here."

"And Adrienne, I am almost thirteen. Do you know when David killed Goliath and became king?"

"No, but I am sure you will tell me."

"He was about thirteen, not much older than I am. And why is my age so important? Why not measure me by my height? I am taller than you are." And suddenly, I too could smile.

Adrienne looked at me intensely, as if I were an unsigned painting to be assessed, her green eyes glaring, and asked, "Well, what is your Goliath, Jacob?"

"The animalcules, the tiny animals that caused the death of my mother, some orphan children I cared for, and a man I met along the Danube."

"Louis Pasteur is a great man, a scholar, a scientist, who loves God and loves his family. He will help you find what you are looking for. But he says you make assumptions that are not backed by science."

"I know about the animalcules, Adrienne. Perhaps I am a savant!"

Suddenly, Adrienne had had enough of me and rose to leave.

"And Adrienne, how old are you?" I asked, proud of my newly found confidence.

"Seventeen, too old for you."

THE SPOILED
WINE OF LILLE

The days and months passed quickly. I had been living in the quarters of the lab assistants. Well, I might say that I was a lab assistant myself. I had an exceedingly small wage but also room and board. I had no financial needs. There were people to talk to, and I could spend the weekends in the vineyards with my father, although I had seldom chosen to do so.

Pasteur and several of his assistants were excited by the new work in the lab. Pasteur had been studying the normal fermentation process of wine for weeks, and his laboratory had made an important discovery—the essential role of living things, yeast, in the fermentation process. However, the laboratory began to look at the spoiled wine and spoiled milk as well. The vineyards of Lille were depending on an explanation for their spoiled, sour wine—an explanation that clearly would not reside in the grapes or vineyards themselves. But Pasteur knew that to understand spoiled wine, he would first have to understand the normal fermentation process. That first step had been completed.

Pasteur spoke to all of the group. "Jacob," he said, "you have the honor of the first look. Search out the yeasts like you have done and see how they fare in the sour wine."

I peered down through the microscope, as I had learned to do in the past. The yeasts were easy to see, and they were still moving and still seemed to be budding.

But I saw what I had seen before in my dreams or my nightmares. I saw what I had imagined, what I had expected to see someday, what I had known must exist in some form but what so many had been unable to see. Through this new instrument that all were worshipping, through the lens of this golden tube, I saw many tiny dots, rodlike or sticklike, tumbling, floating in the wine, in dense families or clusters, dots and dashes, but some longer than others. I saw mostly rods, sausage shaped. They outnumbered the yeasts by far and were much smaller.

I looked up from the microscope and toward the group surrounding me. "I see the cause of the sour wine," I told them.

By the end of the day, numerous specimens of spoiled wine had been reviewed by all the team members. In each case, the tiny creatures overwhelmed the sample. Returning to the normal wine samples, we saw that none had the smaller creatures.

Pasteur wanted to be sure and called for samples of good wine versus spoiled wine. An assistant would place a sample, and an examiner would be asked whether the sample was good or bad without knowing the source. The answer was correct every time. Spoiled wine had the tiny creatures consistently. Finally, after several more weeks of discussion and sample testing, Pasteur gathered the lab group together.

Pasteur stated what we all had come to suspect. "We have seen Leeuwenhoek's animalcules; more recently, Christian Gottfried of Ehrenberg, Germany, has called them 'bacteria,' from the Greek translation of 'little sticks.' Bacteria, living animalcules, have spoiled the wine and destroyed the wine industry of Lille."

Once this conclusion was reached, it was easy to conclude the same for the samples of spoiled milk. The spoiled milk always had the same animalcules, the same bacteria.

I could hardly contain my excitement. "Mr. Pasteur, I believe these creatures were on the hands of the doctors who killed my mother and within the typhus lice that bit and killed the children in my orphanage, and I believe that they killed a man I met in an Austrian farmhouse by entering through the open wound of his leg."

But Pasteur was not moved. "Jacob, you will have to learn that in science you may state your hypothesis, your suspicions. But every hypothesis needs to be proven. Sometimes your suspicions may be correct; at other times they could be proven to be false. What you have suggested may take a lifetime to study, a lifetime to prove. And please, your emotions, your dead friends, must be separate from the laws of logic and the spirit of science."

"Well, Mr. Pasteur, that lifetime I will gladly give up, a lifetime to the study of science."

Pasteur continued to address the group. "Our work is just beginning, and no quick answers are likely to be found. But I will ask you all to think about the meaning of what we have learned today and what we still do not know."

Marie Laurent spoke. "We must learn where the bacteria have come from."

Andre, who was the most learned of the group, proposed the theory of spontaneous generation. "We have known since Aristotle's times that life arises from nonliving matter, such as seen when a fish arises from a new puddle of water or a fly from dead matter or feces. Mice appear from the grain stores in barns, and frogs from the banks of the Nile."

But Marie Laurent, the exceedingly kind woman who had assisted me in adjusting to my quarters, disagreed. She said with a smile, "If these animalcules are living things, just smaller than the eye can see, they likely come from each other, just as a kitten is born from the womb of a mother cat. Perhaps we are seeing such reproduction as the numbers of animalcules increase under the microscope."

Pasteur appreciated the controversy, reveling in the contrasting theories but holding a special affection for the view and person of Marie Laurent. "We will find the answers by determining the appropriate experiments," he said. "When we know where these bacteria come from, we can resolve the spoiled wine problem for Lille, for Luc, for the Bigo vineyard, and for all the winemakers of France."

I was fascinated with this approach to finding such new and valuable information. But I was thinking about the bacteria in a unique way, and I couldn't keep myself from asking another question, even if by asking it I would seem like a silly child. "Mr. Pasteur, should we not think about killing these creatures, these bacteria that spoil wine and bring death to children and mothers?"

"Jacob, you can begin to think about how to kill bacteria in wine without destroying the wine itself."

"Yes, and then later, perhaps how to kill the bacteria in a person without killing the person who has become sick from them."

Pasteur and Marie Laurent looked at each other, and I believe I saw a faint smile.

I hoped I had not said too much.

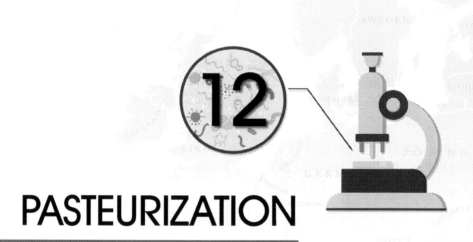

PASTEURIZATION

The laboratory group was at work discussing, reading, and planning for further experiments to determine where the bacteria causing wine spoilage were coming from. Once that determination was made, further studies would be necessary to decide what to do about it. Clearly, the group had already decided we would need many flasks. Flasks were appearing from all sides of the laboratory—wide-mouthed flasks, narrow-mouthed flask, flasks closed at the top, flasks open at the top, flasks with side ports, flasks with multiple arms, flasks with narrow necks that curved downward.

I was learning that the work of science, when done correctly, was tedious. Wrong conclusions could set back progress by years. I was anxious to know about spoiled wine and the solution to its spoilage, but I was more anxious to understand the creatures that had continued to cause my nightmares, creatures that had caused me great sorrow.

I had ideas and visions that I needed to discuss, but I thought I had pressed my luck with Mr. Pasteur and so sought Adrienne to test my views. I also wanted to test my ability to speak with a girl of such beauty about science.

She was in the laboratory as always, planning for the next experiment, when I caught up with her. She held my gaze. I hoped she would not consider me a nuisance.

"Adrienne, when I was in the orphanage, sometimes leftover meat was brought to us. The kitchen team worried that it would spoil since it had been given to us as leftovers from others. So they would quickly cook the meat. In fact, one time some chicken was not well cooked—we could tell that easily—and we all got sick with nausea and vomiting."

"OK, Jacob. I would agree that poorly cooked food can make us all ill."

"And why is that, Adrienne?"

"Obviously, food left out turns bad."

"But why?"

"Jacob, there are so many things we know nothing about, and I suppose that would be one of them."

"But what if we get sick because the creatures, the bacteria, grow in the food?"

She was open to innovative ideas. She did not disregard my comments. "I suppose that would be possible."

She turned her attention to me again in the same way she'd looked at me in my room, and her wide green eyes, red hair, and pale complexion interrupted my thinking process. For a moment, I was not even sure about my name.

I gained my composure and continued. "And perhaps when we heat the food, we kill the bacteria. In this hypothesis, uncooked food would have bacteria in it if conditions were right for the bacteria to grow. Heating the food would kill the bacteria."

"Well, Jacob, you have interesting ideas. Perhaps you should develop some research projects on food safety."

"No, Adrienne, I want to heat the wine to kill the bacteria. I want to heat the milk to kill the bacteria. Perhaps we can save the wine by heating it."

"Wouldn't you destroy the wine by heating it?"

"Yes, I suppose that is a concern that would negate my idea, but maybe there is a temperature, just the right temperature, that would kill the bacteria and leave the wine intact."

Adrienne was a young scientist trained to evaluate hypotheses. She was not about to dismiss me based on my lowly status in the group. "Let us see what Andre has to say about your hypothesis."

Adrienne summarized my ideas for Andre to give them more credibility. Andre, while he might have looked the part of a simple and jolly worker, was in fact most knowledgeable about the work of French scientists and those around the world.

Andre stroked his white beard and nodded intently. He was not about to reject an idea too quickly. He told us that years ago, Napoleon and the French government had offered a financial award to anyone who could find better ways to feed the troops. Nicholas Appert, a Frenchman who had been working on the concept of canning food, described a process of placing food in glass jars, corking the jars, sealing them with wax, and then heating them. This process was adopted and worked well to preserve food for the military and received the award. Of course, no one really knew why it worked.

Adrienne set up a meeting with me, Andre, and Pasteur. Andre made the presentation, a hypothesis that heating the wine could kill the bacteria without destroying the wine or any of its appealing characteristics.

We were all shocked when Pasteur, after listening intently, asked only one question: "At what temperature?"

Andre responded, "We will have to try all temperatures."

Pasteur nodded his approval.

I felt that I must make some contribution. "Mr. Pasteur, if the heating process works, we can call it pasteurization!"

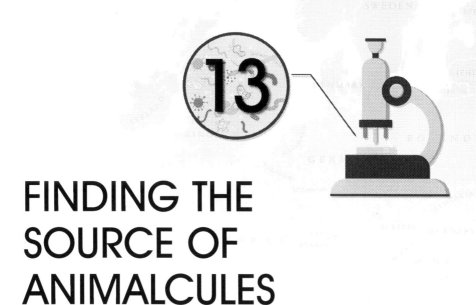

FINDING THE
SOURCE OF
ANIMALCULES

The wines of Lille had become contaminated with bacteria. Of course, that concept was a stunning new revelation not easily believed worldwide. This was not a surprise to me, given that even now, Semmelweis's and my mother's discovery that the hands of physicians caused childbed fever also was not believed. But if bacteria were contaminating the wines of Lille, where were the bacteria coming from?

It was possible that they could be coming from the wine itself or from the soil or from some inanimate matter. But I believed they also could be coming from the growing and dividing bacteria present in the environment. The second possibility was perhaps more concerning—bacteria living and growing everywhere, just ready to cause disease under the right conditions.

The efficiency of the Pasteur lab was more apparent now than ever. Each of six laboratory assistants, including me, had set up a series of flasks. Flask 1 had a broth at its base and a wide neck open to the air. Flask 2 had a long neck bent downward to look like a goose. A third flask also had a gooseneck, but the neck was removed after boiling. Another flask was closed to the air but had piped-in oxygen. At the same time, we began to look for bacteria everywhere—in urine, in spit, in feces. On my own time, I wiped my hands with a wet towel and wrung it into the broth to see if bacteria could be on my hands and thus on the hands of the Vienna physicians.

I would not have believed that these experiments would continue for years, but the concept of spontaneous generation had become entrenched in the minds of scientists from around the world. Spontaneous generation was an accepted scientific principle. The concept had religious and philosophical implications. Where did life come from? And where did bacteria come from?

Bacteria were being seen in flasks filled with broth under some circumstances but not under others. But in summary, after years of study, it was found that nothing grew in the broth in the flasks that were protected from the very air we breathed. Bacteria did not grow in the gooseneck flasks containing broth. Even when the flasks were covered by filters and infused with oxygen, there was no growth in the broth. The broth that was heated and then protected from air did not grow bacteria. Organisms, animalcules, bacteria—whatever you might call these tiny creatures—came from the outside, the air, the environment, and were not generated from the broth itself.

Over two years, the Pasteur laboratory proved that the concept of spontaneous generation, living things growing out of dead material, was not true.

Pasteur presented this finding at some meetings in Paris, and we were told that there was much opposition to the discovery. We saw Pasteur's frustration as he discussed this seeming rejection with many of his lab people. Marie Laurent was particularly supportive and constantly pushed him to continue his work.

This argument on the theory of spontaneous generation would not be resolved for years. I was coming to realize that new ideas often were rejected or in fact opposed with great fervor. Pasteur's reaction to the criticism of his findings reminded me of Herr Semmelweis when he'd described to me the rejection of the childbed fever discovery. At times Pasteur did not look well; the stress of being ridiculed for his scientific breakthroughs was affecting his health.

I saw that Marie Laurent was always at his side during tough times, and I was finally clued in to the fact that Marie was not only Pasteur's favorite assistant but also his wife. They had married the year that I was born.

As our work continued, bacteria were found to be everywhere in the environment, and the implications for their relationship to disease was overwhelming to me. We were a step closer to understanding childbed fever, to understanding typhus, and to understanding why my friend had died from his wound.

If bacteria were abundant in the environment, their relationship to disease was perplexing. We knew that under the right circumstances, bacteria came from the air to a favorable place where they would grow. They could grow in wine, they could grow in broth, and they could grow in urine. And yes, there were bacteria on my hands!

But today Pasteur approached me to discuss our next project—in essence, my project.

"Jacob, we are on to your experiments. We will begin to heat wine at many different temperatures. Let us get the team together to plan the specifics. I will continue these experiments from my home in Arbois. I have worked out methods to heat wine with some instruments there. It is a two-day trip from here, and so I will arrange for your transportation to my home laboratory. It is about time you returned to the vineyards and explained to Luc what we have found and what we are doing. In fact, we will need Luc for some post-boiling wine testing."

It had been many months since I had seen my father or half brother. My return to the vineyard was a vacation from the intense conditions and rigors of the Pasteur laboratory. Pasteur's group was spreading the word around the world that the spoiled wine of Lille had been caused by the long-rumored animalcules, too small to see.

What other problems the bacteria might be causing was for now left unsaid.

Working in the Pasteur laboratory had taught me not only about the principles of science but also about teamwork and relating to others in a way that I had rarely experienced in my twelve years at the Vienna Foundlings. I had thought about all that I had missed out on in never seeing my mother and in never being able to discuss her passions, principles, and aspirations with her. Now I did have the chance to reconnect with my father, a man whom I had met only briefly but who had led me to my great opportunity in life, working with Pasteur.

When I stepped out from my carriage, my father was there to greet me. He was different from those in the laboratory—darker skin, more heavily built, without jacket or vest, dressed in a very simple white cotton shirt bearing the purple stains of the wine business.

"Luc, I am a new person, more confident. I am now fifteen years of age, I believe. I have laboratory training, and I have found my place in the world, at least for now. And although you abandoned me from the very beginning and cared not even to inquire about me, you are still my father, and meeting you was an important step in finding my way in life."

Luc had a way of looking at me that cut through his record of neglect and suggested some caring, sincerity, and regret. "How do we proceed, Jacob? You are my son, but I have no record as your father and no idea how to relate to you. But you are a gifted young person; you look like me but are like your mother. You are welcome to work here in the vineyards with Pierre and me and get back to our business."

"For now," I said with great anticipation, "we have a common goal and a new direction to follow together. We have found the cause of the spoiled wine—animalcules, bacteria."

"Animalcules?"

"They are creatures too small to see, but they live and reproduce and can be found in spoiled wine, but not in good wine. Pasteur and I and others—we made this discovery together. We proved this many,

many times over the past two years. The same is true for spoiled milk. The creatures can be found in spoiled milk as well."

"And how may this discovery help us get our wine business back?"

"We have an idea that heating the spoiled wine may kill the bacteria."

"Heating wine is probably not a good idea!"

"And that is how you and Pierre can help us. We plan to heat wine at many different temperatures in an effort to kill the bacteria but keep the wine's properties intact."

"And how can we help you with this experiment?"

"Obviously, once we heat the wine, we will need you to taste it."

After a weekend of conversation, wonderful food, good wine, and hiking among the green mountains of the vineyard, my father, my half brother, and I took a carriage to Arbois, several hundred miles south of Lille, to begin one of the great experiments of the century.

SAVING THE LILLE WINE INDUSTRY

A rbois was a small city in southern France where the Pasteur family home was located and where the Pasteur family had lived for several generations. The river Cuisance passed through the town, and there had always been a central square that featured townsfolk exhibiting their latest wines and cheeses. The Château Pécauld, built in the eleventh century to defend the city, still stood, a two-story cottage in between pointed towers. Arbois also was where Pasteur had gone to school in a single-room schoolhouse. While he'd started out as a mediocre student, Andre told us, he had won a national physics test contest at age twenty-one and had received his doctorate degree in chemistry at age twenty-four. At age twenty-five, he had become a professor at the University of Strasbourg. Shortly thereafter, he'd received acclaim for a chemistry breakthrough related to the structure of chemical elements. Throughout his busy career, he had always been considered an excellent father and husband. Of course, his early life was inspirational to me.

Our trip to Pasteur's home caused me to reflect on how far I had come thanks to this man. I had been born in 1848, the year that my mother died and Semmelweis commanded the Vienna physicians to wash their hands in chlorine. At age twelve, I had been told of my mother's death and my father's existence. I had set off to find my father, an effort that had taken me on a journey across several countries. Four years had passed since my arrival in France. I looked and thought differently, as one would expect, going as I had from ages twelve to sixteen. Science had become my passion, and Pasteur, my role model. I had learned patience. For years I had been looking at specimens and analyzing results from dawn until dark. On weekends I might go back to the vineyards and hike through the mountains with my stepbrother and father. I couldn't bear to join them in fishing or hunting and must admit that during much of the time I had spent with them, my thoughts had been on the animalcules. But I thanked them for giving me some sense of normalcy, some sense that I was like other people.

In the spoiled wine our laboratory had found animalcules, those creatures that first had been described by Leeuwenhoek, a businessman whose findings had been ignored. I was honored to be part of a team that had confirmed the bacteria suspicion. I wanted to help the vineyards of Lille and my father. But I also wanted to learn about how harmful these creatures might be.

Pasteur met us at the entrance of his home and introduced us to his family. Of course, we knew Marie Laurent, his wife, but for the first time we saw Louis Pasteur as a father. Pasteur had five daughters, including Jeanne, who had died at age nine, and a daughter named Camille who was bedridden with a new acute illness when we arrived and was being attended to by his other daughters.

We were invited into the Pasteur home. It was a three-story brick house with a flat roof, covered in ivy and surrounded by flowerpots and a picket fence. We passed through an office with remnants of the tannery business run by Louis Pasteur's father, who had also been a soldier in Napoleon's army. The home had been redesigned to include a very well-furnished, elegant living room and dining room with colorful curtains and many paintings and sketches. Some of the paintings had been done by Pasteur himself, pastels of his family who had sat as models. There was a portrait of his father, Jean Joseph Pasteur, the tanner, appearing quite sophisticated in a black suit with a thick fur collar and the usual white buttoned shirt of the day.

We traveled down a winding staircase to a large room that easily could have been another elaborate living room, library, and office combination but that, like the Lille laboratory, was filled with flasks, glass tubes, and wooden desks, with books and papers everywhere.

Andre and Adrienne had already set up the lab for the wine experiments. Now the smell of wine was everywhere. Spilled wine could be seen on the floor and desks and clothing.

Spoiled wine had been distributed into twenty different small vats. Each sample had been confirmed to have bacteria under the microscope. The wine vats were immersed in large pools of water that were being heated, causing the temperature in each vat to rise slowly. The temperature was measured by mercury thermometers, starting way below the boiling point at forty degrees centigrade. The data gathering was an arduous process, involving recording the wine temperatures, sampling the heated wine under the microscope, and continuing to review many samples over time. The hope was to find a temperature above which no further bacterial growth would occur in the wine samples. There was great optimism even in the first weeks of the experiments.

Pasteur and Andre reviewed the temperatures to which the wine samples had been heated and examined the wine samples microscopically. Adrienne and I then each reviewed samples under the microscope, not knowing to what temperature each sample had been heated. Andre insisted that there could be no bias in our reports of the quantity of bacteria seen. Luc and Pierre watched our work with interest, waiting for their part in the study.

To say that the work was a remarkable success would be an understatement. To our surprise, bacteria were destroyed easily at a temperature of only fifty degrees centigrade.

Luc and Pierre had brought samples of their most excellent wines to Arbois. The wine samples were heated to fifty degrees centigrade. Luc and Pierre had been tasting wines for most of their adult lives and before. Now they would taste the heated wine after it cooled. All eyes and ears were now on these members of the team.

Luc and Pierre began drinking the samples of wine, samples that had been heated and then cooled. Back and forth, they described their observations in the language of wine lovers, teasing us with a vocabulary of smells and tastes that were beyond our understanding.

"The wines have not been affected by your heating—as much as that does surprise me," said Luc.

"Jacob," said brother Pierre, "you have saved the wine industry of Lille."

Pasteur was a man of few words, a modest man who had helped us learn the beauty of science. "A bottle of wine contains more philosophy than all the books in the world," he said. "As for the animalcules, it is a terrifying thought that life is at the mercy of these minute bodies. It is a consoling hope that science will not be powerless before such enemies."

Listening to Pasteur, I was brought to tears. Adrienne alone recognized my brief loss of emotional control.

Once Pasteur had recorded the results of this experiment, we all celebrated with toasts to the team. Heating wine to fifty degrees centigrade would prevent bacteria from growing in wine samples. The spoiling of wine in Lille, in all of France, would soon end. Similarly, the spoiling of milk and other foods also would someday be prevented and change food safety around the world forever. I had witnessed the birth of pasteurization. This work would be repeated and defined and confirmed many times over many months.

The celebration became a wine tasting event and for me a unique evening, as I had never drunk wine before this night nor appreciated its effects on the psyche. In fact, the beautiful Adrienne and I celebrated together long after all had retired. Now I felt myself to be an adult both in mind and in body. Out of the celebration came new feelings for Adrienne and an idea that she could care for me and I for her. I was encouraged to think that although she was years older than I, she was equally innocent.

Our celebration was cut short the following morning as Pasteur's daughter became increasingly ill. What had started as fever and headache and some stomach pain had progressed to a high fever and very abnormal mental status. A physician was summoned.

I watched at the child's bedside as the doctor ran his fingers over a red, circular skin rash. Then, after tapping his fingers on the child's abdomen, he told me that the liver and spleen were enlarged. "The child has typhoid fever," he said.

Mr. Pasteur was not surprised; he had lost his daughter Jeanne to typhoid when she was only nine years old.

If we had ever doubted that he was just a man, we would doubt no longer. Throughout the night Pasteur wept and prayed. He was a man of faith as well as a man of science, and he made me regret that I had not taken the nuns in the orphanage seriously. He held his wife tightly. He kneeled by his daughter's bedside and spoke to her even when she stopped talking back to him.

As the doctor left the bedside, I had several questions to ask him, and he took the time to listen to me. "So how does one come down with this disease of typhoid fever?"

This young man, nervous, clean-shaven, wearing a white coat and carrying a black bag, answered with some hesitancy and even some sadness. "We are not sure about that, but some have come down with the disease from drinking contaminated water, such as lake water or water that might be contaminated with waste."

"Waste?"

"Like from a stream that has been contaminated with animal or human waste."

"Could this be because of the animalcules in the water?"

"Animalcules?"

"Bacteria?" I hoped that he would understand, but he did not.

"Sorry, not familiar with animalcules. I just recently came out of medical school and know nothing about animalcules," he said with an embarrassed smile.

"And how will we treat this young girl?"

"We can try some turpentine or even some brandy."

"Why those treatments? How do they work?"

"Son, you might make a good medical student, but I don't have those answers for you, and I don't think anyone does. But I will be back to check on her tomorrow."

There was no tomorrow. Camille Pasteur died that night.

Marie and Louis were stunned, silent. They shut us all out from any communication. Louis retired to his bedroom. His sounds of prayer, rage, and distress blended together to remind me of a wounded animal, a sorrow that would be hard to define. Their grief was immense because it was their second child to die from typhoid fever. Because they felt helpless. Because Pasteur was considered a great scientist, a genius, but his knowledge had not been enough to help his own daughter.

I cried too, because my mother had died before I could know her, because I had seen young children die of some other disease with a similar name, because Paul had died although I'd done my best to help him. And I knew from my mother speaking to me from the grave that all of this had to do with animalcules. And the fact that they were too small to see did not make them any less dangerous.

Soon the family was grieving together, and the laboratory assistants who cared so much for their boss were without words and retired to their rooms. Louis Pasteur had not looked well for a long time, but this loss devastated him. The events of the night had left him with red and puffy eyes and pale skin. He looked angry but also dizzy and unwell.

Pasteur could not be consoled, and that was not my primary goal. I needed to speak when others were silent. It was not for me to remain silent.

"Mr. Pasteur, why would a young girl just die like this of some ailment called typhoid fever? Is this an illness that we recognize can cause death in some and recovery in others? If it came from drinking water, what was in the water? Why do the doctors seem to know so little about what they must know to be useful?"

Then, perhaps out of desperation to know what was unknown, I asked about the red-face disease and the question that had always haunted me. "Mr. Pasteur, I saw an outbreak in children of a disease they called measles, a disease all the children had in the orphanage. It spread to everyone, and it came in waves. But those who had the disease were protected from ever getting it again. I believe it is important to know why."

Pasteur wanted to respond even through his grief. "We will answer that question someday, Jacob. And perhaps that principle will guide us in preventing disease in the future. And Jacob, I will never fault you for asking the right questions even if you do so sometimes at the wrong times."

Although Pasteur did not want to hear condolences or speak to anyone, at mid-morning he summoned me.

"Jacob, you have reminded me of myself in many ways. You are smart, as are the others, but you are always asking questions, looking for answers. I know that you are angry when someone dies without explanation. You are obsessed with the animalcules, and you suspect that they are causing some of the diseases that have afflicted us. While it is an assumption on your part, a guess almost, I think you may be right. I have listened to you as you have suspected bacteria of causing your mother's death, your convict friend's wound, and the typhus in the orphanage, and now I know without asking that you will suspect that my child, my children, have also died from bacteria. But Jacob, I am not a physician. I do not understand diseases or diagnoses. I am not an anatomist or a pathologist. The questions you are asking are beyond me. While I am so pleased and proud to have you in my laboratory, you do not belong here. I would like to help you find a physician mentor and even consider a way for you to go to medical school."

But I was not ready to leave the Pasteur lab, not yet. We had just made breathtaking discoveries, and I'd found a life when I had not had one before. I thought about my improving relationship with my father, and I thought about Adrienne.

"Please, sir, for now I would like to stay with you, study with you, and continue my development as a scientist right here—in Lille or in Arbois."

Pasteur, with the saddest of eyes, agreed. In fact, I think he was glad to know that I was sticking around.

Months after the death of Pasteur's daughter, I received a letter from Vienna—my first contact with my former life, a letter from Neil. While I was pleased to hear of Neil's success from the letter, I now had to mourn two additional deaths.

Dear Jacob,

It has been five years, but I hope you still remember me as Neil, your orphanage friend. I have been working with Dr. Hebra, whom you may remember meeting in the orphanage with Dr. Semmelweis. You will be pleased to know I have become a medical student under Hebra, and we are studying a new field called dermatology, describing and categorizing all of the different skin problems that we used to see in the orphanage. We have learned much about measles, typhus, and other such diseases. They are much less controversial than childbed fever. Eventually, I will be a pediatrician and the doctor for the orphanage.

We both saw an article about your important work with Mr. Pasteur in the vineyards.

Dr. Hebra gave up the childbed fever work long ago, as did all the others. The hand-washing basin is gone. We wanted you to know that Dr. Semmelweis has died. His behavior had become more and more erratic as the years went on, and recently he could no longer care for himself. Dr. Hebra, with a heavy heart, was forced to arrange his admission to an asylum. Shortly after admission, he died. Rumor has it that he may have been beaten, but at autopsy he had a wound on his wrist that might have been due to the erosion of his restraints. They told us that in his delirium prior to death he would call out the name of your mother and once called your name as well. Hebra believes that your work with Pasteur may in fact be shedding light on the true cause of childbed fever. Do you think the poison on the hands of doctors may actually be the same animalcules that cause wine to spoil?

Unfortunately, I write you to give you more sad news. Our dear friend Gedeon is also dead. He left the orphanage a few years after you did. He hoped to change Viennese society and speak for all the children so mistreated at the Vienna Foundlings, but society here was not ready to listen to a young orphan. He believed so passionately in equal treatment for all, for the right of all to equal opportunity. Unlike you and I, he was outraged by the lack of opportunity for the children at the Foundlings. He spoke of democracy and read extensively about the United States Constitution. You remember his cunning; well, somehow, he found a way to stow away on a ship to America.

I learned that he joined the Union army to fight for the principles he believed in. He was only nineteen. Imagine wanting to fight for a country of which you are not even a citizen. Gedeon died in the battle of Gettysburg. I was listed as his next of kin and was informed that he survived a serious gunshot wound that required amputation. Months later, the gangrene surrounding the amputation site could not be controlled, and he died of its complications.

I have another important message for you. Your mother had a close friend, a nurse Hannah, who was with her when she died. She was the one who called first for Kolletschka, and then Semmelweis, to quickly come to your mother's bedside. Hannah was there when your mother made her final wishes.

Hannah had seen me a few times in the hospital wards and knew I had grown up in the orphanage, and she wondered if I had known you. Although it is many years later, she regrets that she never came to the Foundlings to speak with you. Your mother had been adamant that you would need no visitors, no sponsors, and no special support. She believed that you would develop resilience and character in the Foundlings just as she had done. But Hannah never accepted her own lack of involvement with you. She wanted you to know that your mother was more than a doctor and scientist. She had overcome unspeakable obstacles as an orphan, a medical student, and the first women obstetrician in Vienna. She had battled her male colleagues to eventually become their thought leader. But while she would take great pride in your scientific achievements, she would also want you to live your life with more joy, more love of life than she was ever able to have. Hannah knows that your mother would want you to be successful in finding the happiness in life that she never found.

You were right about many things—the orphanage did make us stronger, and we are still able to experience joy like others who had parents.

By the way, we do have a microscope now, but I have not found any microbes in the measles rashes.

Jacob, I do hope we meet again as friends someday.

MEETING NAPOLEON

The successes of the Pasteur laboratory only intensified the group's appetite for further successes. The death of Pasteur's daughter heightened our interest in applying research principles to the prevention and treatment of diseases, especially those that were caused by animalcules, or what some were now calling germs. To me, identifying and categorizing the types of animalcules was of most interest. However, fate would lead us to a new battleground—a study that would last for years and take me away from my research interest yet lead us to save France again.

When Pasteur told Adrienne and me to prepare for a trip to the Château de Fontainebleau just outside of Paris, our destination's significance was lost on me. That the palace had been home to Louis VII and all subsequent kings of France meant little to a Viennese orphan. But by the time we had learned about the special carriage that was to bring us to the palace, received instructions on how to dress, and even had a discussion of what would be said about the fermentation of the wine discovery, I knew that this was a major step even in the life of Pasteur himself.

Much of the palace decor was said to be unchanged from the beginning of the 1100s through the reigns of King Louis and the Napoleons. The palace was flanked by a courtyard and huge garden. There were ornamental vases and sculptures of ancient-looking figures. Immense flowerbeds and fruit trees surrounded the palace. Upon entrance to the palace, we saw imperial emblems in gold and white painted on the walls. There were huge wooden eagle sculptures and additional sculptures representing symbols of glory, justice, and abundance. The ceiling was as high as I had ever seen, with decorative columns surrounding the room. The floors were of shining wood but were covered completely with rugs, all with multicolored flower patterns, mostly pink and purple. The chairs, also in pink or purple, were of a size suitable for giants, as were the fireplaces. The chandeliers, made of beaded glass and with gold trim along their circumference, were large and circular, extending from the large ceiling halfway to the floor.

We were ushered into a massive theater to be met with a grand reception. The diplomatic world was represented by the ambassador to Russia and Prussia, a Dr. Longet, who had written a treatise on physiology; Paul Baudry, a famous French painter; and the novelist Jules Sandeau. We were all congratulated for the scientific discoveries that had saved the French wine industry. This was a distinguished group of Frenchmen, all standing around with wine glasses in hand, individuals slowly moving across the room and forming groups in which to converse, but with new groups constantly reforming. I had begun to realize that while I was an expert at discussing science, microscopes, and germs, I was at a loss when it came to politics, the war, or the economy of Europe.

Each guest stayed the night in a luxurious room, and the next morning, Emperor Napoleon III asked for a private visit with the three of us. Pasteur knew to bring his microscope and some samples of spoiled wine. The empress joined us and enthusiastically invited her entourage to listen to Pasteur's short and simple account of our discoveries and to look through the eyepiece of the microscope and see germs.

But this invited visit was not just about past achievements. Pasteur would be asked again to save a French industry, this time the silkworm industry—and the request would be made by Napoleon III himself. My life would be turned away from disease and toward worms, moths, eggs, and chrysalides.

Napoleon III cut a memorable image. His hair was black, combed back, and thick on the sides. He had a black beard that came to a point, and his mustache also ended in a point on both sides. He was short but probably taller than his grandfather. He wore a white cape, white pants with black boots, and a red vest over a black shirt. He looked like someone who might be in an orphanage theater rehearsal. But he was not intimidating at all. In fact, he was quite friendly and began by telling us he had an interest in science and microscopes.

"We are honored to be here, Emperor, and I am pleased to see you again," said Pasteur. "I would like to introduce my two most valued assistants. Adrienne has been with me from the beginning of my work at Lille. She may take over my laboratory once I am retired. Jacob is a true genius, one who has had great intuition about the study of animalcules."

I had to quickly recuperate from the brief introduction. I had not realized that I was thought to be a genius or that Adrienne would become the next leader of the Pasteur laboratories. My thoughts had been leaning toward the assumption that Adrienne might stay in Lille forever while I was destined to move to wherever the war against bacteria was most focused. Of course, neither of us was particularly good at dealing with issues involving feelings or long-term relationships. My thoughts were interrupted when I heard my name.

"Jacob, then, from which university have you developed such expertise?" asked the emperor.

"Sir, I have not really gone to school anywhere, although I did read and learn at my orphanage in Vienna. I must admit, I did not expect to speak with a Napoleon, ever."

"Well, I appreciate a man who is self-made, much like my own family. And have you played a role in the great salvation of our wine industry?"

"Yes, sir, I did suggest that the wine might be heated to destroy the germs and still maintain its taste. I also helped to show that germs are everywhere, even on our own hands, and that they reproduce from each other just like other animals and not from the soil or excrement. In fact, my own mother died because physicians did not wash their hands during deliveries. Animalcules are everywhere, sir, and if you drink sour milk, you will get sick because you will be swallowing germs. It is my belief that the different diseases you know, such as typhus, food poisoning, typhoid, and leg wounds, are all caused by germs, and probably each disease is caused by a different germ."

Pasteur, with an embarrassed smile, rushed in quickly to say, "Jacob always has interesting ideas that he knows he will spend many years trying to prove."

"Jacob, I must ask you then," said the emperor, "what is your intuition about the death of our silkworms?"

"Well, I have not studied silkworms yet. But I will be incredibly happy to do so. Perhaps they too are being killed by the animalcules. We should look not only at the worms but also at their eggs and all their other stages of development under the microscope, to see what the differences between a healthy and sick worm look like. If there are germs causing their illness, we will find them."

Napoleon seemed elated by this answer accompanied by such bravado and said, "And Mr. Pasteur, may I assume this young man will lead the silkworm team?"

"Yes, of course, Jacob is the man who will save the silkworm industry in France," Pasteur said with a smile.

Pasteur then looked at me with seriousness, with his most intense look, narrowing his eyes and protruding his snub nose as if to say, "Get it done."

SAVING THE
SILKWORMS

While Pasteur had agreed to come to Alais in southern France to solve the silkworm problem at the request of Napoleon III, he was unsure of his ability to do so. To a colleague who was enthusiastic about his participation, he wrote: "The proposition is indeed most flattering, and the object is a high one. But it troubles and embarrasses me. Remember if you please that I have never even touched a silkworm!" J. B. Dumas, a political leader of the region, wrote to Pasteur: "A mysterious disease is destroying the silkworm nurseries. Eggs, worms, chrysalides, moths—the disease may manifest in all of them. Whence does it come, and how is it contracted? No one knows, but its invasion is manifest by little black spots and therefore called corpuscle disease."

The problem was ruining the silkworm business in France, Italy, Spain, and Austria. The European economy depended on silkworms. Millions of dollars had been lost because the silkworms were oddly dancing and dying. Hypotheses for the silkworm demise included atmospheric conditions, degeneration of the race of silkworms, inferior-quality mulberry trees, and many more.

Pasteur wanted Adrienne and me, and others as needed, to take the lead on this project. At age twenty, I was no longer the young boy who'd arrived at the laboratory with just ideas, a strong work ethic, and no laboratory skills. Pasteur had many other issues on his mind, particularly defending his rejection of the theory of spontaneous generation around Europe and continually grieving for his daughter.

Pasteur was to accompany us to Alais for a day or two. But the night before we left, he became ill. Ever since the death of his daughter, he had not seemed well. While meeting with us, he briefly lost his ability to speak, and his left arm became weak. This gave us great concern, but it lasted but a few seconds, and then he was back to being himself. Nevertheless, he decided that we should leave without him.

The next morning, as we prepared to say goodbye, we found him to be much worse and barely able to walk. The episode the night before had been a warning attack. By the light of the next day, he had had a stroke. To see this man who had always seemed so indestructible so afflicted was devastating to both Adrienne and me. We postponed our visit to Alais and summoned Pasteur's physician.

Along with his wife, we held a vigil by his bedside. Pasteur, recognizing the signs of a stroke, accepted this fate with some equanimity. As for us, we pondered the role of stress in his life as his many breakthroughs were being met with some disbelief, jealousy, and even hostility. Europe was not prepared to reject the principle of spontaneous generation, just like it could not accept the concept of childbed fever being caused by physicians' hands. Grief over his daughter's death had also changed him. I thought about the demise of Semmelweis and wondered why new ideas had to take such a toll on those breaking new ground.

Pasteur's physician arrived quickly and prescribed fourteen leeches to be attached to his left ear. I continued to be fascinated with the work of physicians and saw them as somewhere between barbers and true scientists, and I was able to have a word with the doctor as he left the patient.

"The leeches—how will they help Mr. Pasteur improve?"

"It is just the accepted treatment of the day. I presume that it will decrease the amount of blood in his body and improve his circulation."

"Is it that he has too much blood in his body, and if so, why not just remove some by entering a vein?"

The doctor looked at me with a puzzled expression and asked, "Why would you question an accepted treatment?"

Again, I was disappointed in this profession. However, within two days Mr. Pasteur had improved, although he would continue to have some long-term weakness. When his doctor returned for the follow-up examination and removed the leeches, he sought me out to say, "You should have more faith in your mentor's doctor."

I had to respond, not meaning at all to be disrespectful or ungrateful, "But might he have improved anyway, just on his own?"

Pasteur, looking much better but for a sore ear, bade Adrienne and me to head to Alais and find out what was wrong with the silkworms.

We arrived in Alais after a carriage ride that I might have considered romantic based on the books that I had read. Both of us continued to struggle with the idea that we had begun to go down a path of romantic involvement seemingly so normal and natural in others.

We went right to work because we were now a team, a team that represented a great scientist who might someday be recognized around the world. Adrienne and I began by speaking with those who were working in the silkworm nurseries. The disease of the silkworms had been called pebrine, and the original thought was that it had something to do with the brown corpuscles, the brown spots seen on the afflicted caterpillars. Adrienne and I quickly came to understand the metamorphosis process of silkworms. Moths laid eggs, from which silkworms hatched. These silkworms were fed mulberry leaves until they shed their hides. They then built cocoons of silk that came from their heads. The cocoons were dipped into hot water so that the silkworms would die before breaking the cocoon of silk that they had made. But of late, the worms had developed brown spots and appeared dizzy, uncoordinated, and unable to produce silk.

We introduced ourselves to the cultivators of silk, a dozen or so men dressed in various colored berets and kerchiefs. They all appeared similarly sullen, not truly understanding our role.

We asked them what had been learned or done so far to combat the pebrine. Dusting the worms with charcoal and sulfur and spraying them with alcohol had been fruitless. The only clue to the disease was that the sick worms often had brown corpuscles speckled along their torso. The group did not seem happy with our being there, and we were not about to tell them that Napoleon had sent us.

Their apparent leader, an older man, burly, unkempt, very tan, and distinct with a white beret, stepped forward to speak to us. "When we asked the government for help, we did not expect it to send two teens to solve our pebrine problem. Are you sure you have come to the right place?"

"Yes, sir," said Adrienne. "We represent Mr. Pasteur, who is too ill to travel today, and we plan to use the field of science to understand the problem, to identify what is killing your silkworms."

I continued, "Just as small animalcules, too small to see, destroyed the wines in Lille, it is possible that such animalcules are killing the silkworms."

My comments were greeted by amusement but also with some interest; after all, the livelihood of this group depended on us. If we found a solution to the deaths of the silkworms, we would go from being odd youngsters to industry heroes.

Adrienne and I set up our laboratory with a microscope for each of us, and just as we had looked at the normal and diseased wines, we began to look at the silkworms—with and without corpuscles. The silkworm cultivators filled our laboratories with healthy and sick worms, as we had requested. The two of us worked together in a very pleasant, even glorious way despite the worms all around us. We saw the dense oval corpuscles in most of the sick worms but rarely in the healthy ones. We followed the sick worms over time and found that they developed more and more of the corpuscles.

In the evenings we would discuss what our microscopic findings meant. To me the corpuscles were animalcules, although admittedly not bacteria. Bacteria got their name from the Greek translation "sticks," and what we saw were clearly not sticks. They were also larger than the bacteria that I had seen in wine, in broth, and on my hands. I knew that they were alive, for they could be seen budding off or reproducing one from the other. Adrienne did not want to assume that these living creatures were the ones killing the worms but postulated that they were dying from a poison instead. But just as I knew that it had not been a poison on the hands of the Vienna physicians that caused the death of those women, I believed that these silkworms were not dying from a poison. After a week of looking at sick and healthy worms and sick and extremely sick worms, we set out to do some additional experiments.

We placed very sick worms on mulberry leaves. These sick worms had many brown spots on them that one could see with the naked eye. They also moved and danced in unusual ways, not like healthy worms. We then removed the sick worms from the leaves and put healthy worms on the same leaves. The healthy worms soon got sick, and after just a few days they were clearly, visibly sick, with the corpuscles easily seen.

Next, we looked at the silkworm eggs; some of them also were riddled with corpuscles. We waited for the eggs to hatch, and when they did, we found that the larvae were sick. Even when studying moths under the microscope, we could distinguish the sick from the well.

We communicated the results to Pasteur by letter. I was ready to heat the moths to see if we could kill the animalcules and leave the moths intact but agreed that doing so would likely not be practical. Rubbing the larvae with varying substances had already been tried by the cultivators.

I remembered the typhus outbreak in the orphanage. Just keeping the children isolated from any sick person had been a way to end the problem. Adrienne agreed that after each set of eggs was laid, we would examine the parent worms for corpuscles—if they were present, we would destroy the eggs; if not, we would keep the eggs in a protected collection. Eventually, we would have only healthy eggs and then healthy silkworms.

Over several months, our method seemed to work well, and we celebrated our success, our great teamwork, and our superb relationship. We worked hard to help the industry separate the sick from the well worms, even having the cultivators learn to use the microscopes themselves until the sick worms started to disappear.

As the silkworm industry improved, we had an unexpected setback. Just when we had a scientifically proven solution, we were confronted by the cultivators with some additional sick worms. To our great surprise, these sick worms did not have corpuscles or eggs with corpuscles, but they were just as sick. The group was not happy, nor were we. Science could be exhilarating but also disappointing.

Adrienne and I went back to our microscope work, but we could not find corpuscles anywhere. The worms were sick, and they danced their sad dance, but there were no corpuscles in the eggs or moths or worms.

However, as we studied every inch of their bodies, we found that the insides of the worms looked different, and after some dissection, we found bacteria—sticks—that we had never seen in normal silkworms. These silkworms that were sick did not have corpuscles, but they did have bacteria. In fact, we had found that there were two different animalcules causing two different diseases.

My time spent in Alais with Adrienne had brought me to two important conclusions. While silkworms had taken me away from the diseases of man, they had taught me important lessons about disease. I remained overly excited about finding ways to kill the animalcules. However, preventing disease and protecting the healthy from the sick was another path to fighting disease. And if there was a possibility that multiple animalcules were causing disease in silkworms, surely the same must also hold true for humans.

Second, I had concluded that Adrienne and I should work together indefinitely, spending our lives together, but I was unsure of how to prove that hypothesis. I regretted that I had mentors in science but not in the lessons of life itself.

LETTER FROM LISTER

continued my work with Louis Pasteur for seven years and grew from a mature twelve-year-old to an almost-twenty-year-old accomplished scientist—though, granted, an individual with no formal training and little life experience. I was with a great man and a great scientist. Together we had saved the wine industry, discovered the process of pasteurization, proved the germ theory, and solved the problem of the dying silkworms. We continued to study the bacteria in sour milk and patented the pasteurization process. One evening, unbeknownst to the others, I myself drank sour milk that had a particularly substantial number of bacteria in microscopic samples. Because I had been told many times that such an action would be beneath a true scientist, I kept the matter to myself when I became ill with nausea, vomiting, and diarrhea.

I had convinced myself that bacteria caused disease, and while I continued to love Louis Pasteur, I also knew that what Louis Pasteur had told me years ago was becoming increasingly true. I wanted to study disease in a hospital, and I wanted to learn to kill bacteria and cure sick people. I wanted to become a doctor, but a good one who would know how to fight disease and how to take care of people based on facts and science. I wanted to in some way avenge the death of my mother and follow in her footsteps.

My life changed again when Mr. Pasteur summoned me to read a letter he had just received:

My dear sir,

Allow me to beg your acceptance of a pamphlet, which I have sent by the same post, containing an account of some investigations into the subject that you have done so much to elucidate, the germ theory. I flatter myself that you may read with some interest what I have written about organisms which you were the first to describe. If so, you will have seen a description of an antiseptic system of treatment that I have been laboring with for the last nine years to bring to perfection. Allow me to take this opportunity to tender you my most cordial thanks for having with your brilliant researchers demonstrated to me the truth of the germ theory, and thus furnished me with the principle upon which antiseptic treatment can be carried out. Should you at any time visit Edinburgh, it would give you sincere gratification to see at our hospital how largely mankind is being benefitted by your labors. Forgive the freedom with which a common love of science inspires me. Yours very sincerely,

Dr. Joseph Lister
Glasgow, Scotland, 1867

Dr. Pasteur responded on the same day.

Dear Dr. Lister,

Thank you for your compliments about our work. To know that I have moved your important studies forward is a great source of satisfaction to me. But I am writing this letter to introduce you to an extraordinary young man who I would like to suggest might be of assistance to you as a research assistant. Please permit me to take some pages to describe this individual. His name is Jacob Pfleger. He is twenty years old but quite remarkable, perhaps a savant but definitely a genius. He has a strong intuition in a particular domain, and like your David Hume from Edinburgh has said, a genius is often quite disconnected from society due to devotion to his work. Jacob may have been traumatized by hearing about the death of his mother to childbed fever. He has also seemed to get involved with disease and death in his orphanage, but also more recently, he shared in the mourning of my daughter who died before our eyes of typhoid fever. He is often proven correct about hypotheses that he actually does not have the data to support.

Jacob is obsessed with the animalcules that he assumes caused the death of his mother. Since then, he has seen these animalcules everywhere and dreams about them in his sleep. He was quite correct in helping to make the initial observation of the animalcules ruining the fermentation of wines in Lille and later suggested that heating the wine at just the right temperature would solve the problem. He also led the investigation that disproved the spontaneous generation theory, showing that indeed bacteria or animalcules were everywhere and did not come out of inert environment. He has independently studied the bacteria that are on his own hand. He led the investigation of the dying silkworms in Alais and found two separate diseases, likely caused by germs. At times I fear he would jeopardize his own life to find the truth about his animalcules.

I write this letter to you because as much as I value Jacob's work, he has become increasingly impatient and unhappy in our lab. He told me that he is done studying wine and silkworms. He wants to categorize bacteria and find specific ways to kill them. I am not a physician, and my expertise is in finding new treatment, although I am interested in methods of prevention of disease. Jacob is very excited to work with you, find bacteria in surgical specimens, and develop methods to eradicate them. I am quite willing to provide the funds for his travel and relocation to Glasgow. For the good of our science, I hope you will accept my offer.

Louis Pasteur

Dr. Lister's reply soon arrived.

Dear Sir,

It would be a privilege to accept Jacob as a lab assistant here in Scotland. My group is depending more and more on microscopy in our study of wounds, and his experience will be invaluable. Many years ago, I was visiting Vienna on my honeymoon and stopped at the Vienna Medical School to give a lecture on surgical technique. I was interested in the Semmelweis theory of sterility and had a chance to speak with Semmelweis himself. At the very time we were speaking, a young boy came up to us and waited for his turn to speak with Semmelweis. It was quite curious that a young boy would be at such a conference, and I asked the boy who he was. He told me that doctors had killed his mother because they had not washed their hands. For some reason, just as I have not forgotten Semmelweis, I have always remembered the strange encounter with the boy. I believe that it may be the same Jacob.

Joseph Lister, MD

ADRIENNE AND GLASGOW

What had begun as a search for my father and my identity had become instead an opportunity to follow my dream of learning about disease, the cause of my mother's death, and the role of animalcules in causing illness. I had learned that challenging work and the right questions could unlock many of the mysteries of this world and that our ignorance related to disease was everywhere. It was like we were just now beginning to understand the world we lived in.

Finding my father and even a half brother had been a joy. They had helped me to understand that the average person was not driven as I was by the need to understand, was not plagued with nightmares to learn what we did not know. Most, in fact, found their joy in hiking over rolling hills, appreciating a good wine, and finding some suitable mates. Fate had brought me to Lille not to meet my father but to meet Mr. Pasteur and learn the methods of science. The spirit of my mother had somehow guided my way. Now, after so many years of working in the Pasteur laboratories, I knew that I must move on. I hoped to collaborate with doctors like Dr. Lister, not just to identify bacteria but to begin to destroy them forever.

Adrienne, like me, had lived in a bubble of science and work ethic. Our life together had transpired in various laboratories where wine or worms had been what tied us together. As I left for Glasgow, I had to either say goodbye or ask her to come with me.

I met her in her laboratory office. There were no romantic sites for us. Her college diploma and several academic award certificates were mounted on the walls of this tiny office adjacent to the vast new government-supported laboratories of the Pasteur program. She was an only child who had told me nothing about her family. Her past had been a mystery to me, a topic she had chosen not to discuss. She had played a key role in the organization of the Pasteur laboratory. She had always hypnotized me with her reddish-orange hair and penetrated my soul with her green eyes. Scotland was a complicated trip, so I saw the future in a simple way—she might choose to come with me, or we would part.

The task, my plea, became less difficult than I had expected.

"Jacob, I will miss you so. You are as pure a person as there could ever be, and there may be no one smarter or more gifted than you. You are born to change the world and see what our new germ theory means for mankind. I am just another scientist, but one who has had the opportunity to work in the greatest laboratory in Europe. I have no skill or inclination to be a doctor or to help Dr. Lister study disease at his surgical hospital. So before you say anything else, let us agree to go our separate ways with continued love for each other."

"Adrienne, you are a scientist, and I hope that I too have become one. But do you understand the meaning of what you say—of continued love for each other?"

"There are many things you don't know about me. You like my hair, my eyes, my face. You like that I am a scientist, and we surely have had great, unusual experiences together, but you don't know me, and probably that is for the better."

"I can learn more about you every day, every year—your family, your childhood."

"What type of family life would we have, and what do you know about raising children?" she asked sadly.

"Well, I could just depend on you to get me through what I do not understand."

That comment seemed to bring her to tears. "Jacob, my life is not like studying a microbe. There are many things you could never understand, including the loyalty to Pasteur that I must continue to have."

I assumed she was right. There were so many things in life I had not been taught. She did not want to marry an orphan. I thought about staying with Pasteur, giving up my next steps in the microbe war to continue my relationship. But it was a sacrifice I couldn't make. I had come too far to stop now. My loyalty did not extend as far as hers did.

Perhaps if we had had closer family members or better friends, we might have gotten useful advice about this dilemma. I'd left Vienna alone seven years earlier, and I would leave France for Glasgow alone as well.

My other goodbyes were not as difficult. My dad and half brother were a joy but not part of my life script. And Louis Pasteur would be a daily inspiration and a source of constant communication as we studied germs, each in our own way.

Traveling from Paris to Glasgow was not at all like my journey to Lille seven years prior. Having Pasteur's financial support enabled me to negotiate the much-improved train service, the ferry, and the coach to Glasgow in less than one week.

Edinburgh had been the capital of Scotland since the fifteenth century. The city was a leader not only in science and medicine but also in law and education. There was a Royal College of Physicians and a Royal College of Surgeons established by a royal charter. It had a history of cultivating great thinkers, and Dr. Joseph Lister was among them. The Royal Infirmary, where Lister worked, and the University of Edinburgh, where he lectured, were leading centers of medicine in Europe. Lister had moved from Edinburgh to Glasgow to become the professor of surgery at the University of Glasgow and a surgeon at the Glasgow Infirmary. Glasgow had grown to be much larger than Edinburgh and was becoming a leader in complex surgeries and surgical trauma.

Lister's assistants were excellent hosts, and I realized that I had brought with me from France the respect that came from being a colleague of Pasteur.

I was directed into a large operating theater. There were hundreds of spectators waiting to hear an important message from their chief of surgery. Lister was young and dapper, as I remembered him from Vienna. He had not aged, and he demanded respect when he entered a room. He walked into the surgical theater at the same time as assistants, house surgeons, and even young operating room staff. There were doctors, surgeons of all ages, filling all levels of the room, even the top galleries. Lister's surgeons were young, confident, and collegial among themselves.

I did not know whether Lister knew that his assistants had met me at my new quarters and directed me to attend this event. To my surprise, he introduced me as the new research assistant from the laboratory of Louis Pasteur and proceeded to give an address on the issue of postsurgical complications, which had been increasingly problematic in Scotland and around Europe. More surgeons were being trained, and more excellent techniques had been developed. But more and more cases were being plagued by postsurgical complications, or putrefaction as the surgeons called it. Many patients, half of all cases, were left with limbs that were pus-filled or developed serious skin infections. Sometimes, over time the wound would develop a large accumulation of pus that could be easily drained. Sometimes the inflammation would spread up the leg or arm and then to the face or abdomen with no opportunity for drainage. Sometimes the wound would smell terrible and turn black or green. Often the patient would die. Lister reported that there had been sixteen deaths out of thirty-four recent surgical cases in the Edinburgh hospital. He began his address:

"As I have recently written in the journal *Lancet*, the germ theory supplies us with the nature and habits of the subtle foe we have to contend with; and without a firm belief in the truth of the germ theory, perplexity and blunders must be of frequent occurrence. The facts upon which the germ theory is based appear sufficiently convincing. We know from the research of Pasteur and his colleagues that the atmosphere does contain floating particles and spores of minute vegetations. The septic energy of the air is directly proportional to the abundance of the minute organisms in it and can be destroyed entirely by means of calculations to kill its living organisms—as, for example, through exposure to high temperature. Hence, we cannot refuse to believe that these living animalcules are associated with and indeed the cause of surgical putrefactive complications. And the chief agents in this process appear to be animalcules endowed with the faculty of locomotion, so that they are able to make their way speedily along a layer of fluid such as pus. Admitting, then, the truth of the germ theory and proceeding in accordance with it, we must destroy the organisms that may exist in the part concerned. Upon these principles, a trustworthy treatment for fractures and wounds must be established for the first time."

There was only silence in the room. Lister was suggesting that the reason so many patients died after surgical procedures was that germs were getting into their wounds, that germs were actually raining down from the operating room environment into the surgical field—that these complications of inflammation, pus, fever, and death were preventable! I thought about the negative reaction to and disbelief of the Semmelweis hand-washing breakthrough and the negative reaction to the Pasteur germ theory, and I knew that Lister would be facing a wave of hostility, disbelief, and mistrust after this address. Just as physicians could not accept that their hands were the cause of childbed fever, how would surgeons accept that they were killing patients by inviting germs into their operative wounds?

I knew that I had arrived in Scotland for a reason and that if I was committed to the fight against germs, for now, this was the place to be. I did not understand that my new environment would soon include not just working with germs under the microscope but also working with blood-filled surgical fields, collaborating with a new type of colleague, viewing gaping wounds, seeing desperately sick patients, navigating surgical complications, and confronting death.

THE GLASGOW SURGEONS

I was given a small office in the Glasgow Royal Infirmary about forty miles outside of Edinburgh. The combined office and laboratory included two microscopes similar to what I had been used to in France. For me, the work with Lister was a new life, chaotic with the coming and going of hospital personnel, doctors, patients, and nurses. I had to get used to the shouting, even screaming, of those in pain, including children and worried parents. There were patients wrapped in bandages or walking with crutches, patients who seemed confused, and others who were seemingly in deep sleep. The people I encountered mostly were waiting to see a doctor or a nurse or to have an operation performed. For the sake of this opportunity, I adapted to this new, chaotic environment.

For the first time—well, really the second time if I included Vienna—I met with Dr. Lister, who was surrounded by his young group of surgeons. He was tall and dressed in a black suit, white shirt, and even a bowtie. His hair was black but starting to gray, with very thick tufts extending downward past his cheeks and around his chin and even hanging down over his collar. Otherwise, he appeared very neat and very fit, and he bounded into my office with great energy. He was outgoing and personable, with a personality different from Mr. Pasteur's. He always seemed like he was in a hurry. He spared me a reference to our first meeting in Vienna, and he made it clear to his group that, as young as I was, I was a person to be respected, the representative of a great European laboratory.

"Gentlemen, recognize our braw laddie, our new colleague, Jacob." Turning to me, he continued, "Jacob, all of us are here that we may be enabled in the treatment of patients with a single eye to their good. You will find it hard to understand that all of us are in love with the discipline of surgery. We have a high degree of enjoyment every day, experiencing this bloody and butchering department of the healing arts. But as we do more complicated and lifesaving surgery, saving people from accidents and trauma, so many of our surgical incisions go bad. When we expect to see healing, we often see pus draining from our incisions, incisions that won't close, large spreading skin involvement, and often gangrene and foul-smelling drainage."

One of the surgeons, Dr. Cameron, the youngest, blondest, and most articulate, jumped in as if offended by Lister's remarks. "Mate," said Dr. Cameron, "but we have always believed, and most of us still believe, that these problems are inevitable and not the result of our surgical technique or our methods. The oxygen in the air is not good for boggin' tissue. Oxygen breaks down the molecules of the body's muscle and skin tissue, turning them into pus. There is no way to keep oxygen from a wound or to prevent putrefaction."

I knew to say nothing. Lister responded calmly, perhaps like the many religious leaders he had grown up with, respectfully but with a sincere readiness to fight against well-entrenched surgical dogma.

"Jacob is no wee barra. This young man from the laboratory of the barry Louis Pasteur is now part of our surgical team. The world is turning in a new direction. The primary source of contamination from the air may not be oxygen but invisible, clarty particles from the air, particles that are alive and able to multiply but also particles that we must now call animalcules, or better still the word derived from the Germans—bacteria. Jacob has seen these bacteria, studied them, and determined that they were responsible for the spoiling of wine and deaths of silkworms."

"Naw, Joseph," said Dr. Cameron. "Please, is there not a significant difference between our surgical patients, wine, and silkworms?"

The rest of the group nodded their approval of his skepticism.

"Jacob, perhaps you can answer this important question," Lister stated with confidence.

To speak to surgeons, doctors who took care of patients, to explain to them what I had come to suspect and know—this was my destiny. But I needed to choose my words carefully. I was no longer a child. I would not say that doctors had killed my mother because they had not washed their hands. I would use the term *bacteria* and not *animalcules*. I would start with the facts only and not my assumptions, assumptions that I nevertheless knew to be true.

"Bacteria are everywhere we work and live. We can see them under the microscope, and we can show them to you. They are in the air but will settle in any organic material. They can be found on the hands of anyone, including physicians, and can be transferred into a wound or even into a woman after a pelvic exam. And while we know that they can kill silkworms, it is an assumption hanging in the balance that they can kill patients. I know that bacteria are in soured milk and that drinking such bacteria-laden milk will make one sick. Bacteria may be the cause of typhus, of typhoid fever, of measles, and of your bad results in surgery." The last comment caused a visual grimace. I again had gone too far. "Since air can't be kept from a wound, we must find a way to destroy the animalcules—rather, the germs, the bacteria—that are falling from the air into the surgical wounds."

Lister interrupted. "Pure, dead brilliant. If the wound could be treated with some substance that without doing mischief to the tissues would kill the germs, then putrefaction could be prevented."

I continued, "If we could determine what germs cause what infections, we might then develop specific poisons to kill the germs without hurting the patients."

Lister agreed, putting his arm around me and stating, "Just as we may destroy lice on the head of a child with poisonous applications that will not injure the scalp, so I believe we can use poisons on wounds to destroy bacteria without injuring the soft tissue of the patients."

Lister continued, "Gentlemen, join me in this great trial, a trial that will change surgery forever. Let us begin to identify and destroy bacteria that are harming our patients and destroying our precise surgical technique and let us begin now."

That night, as I lay in my new quarters within the hospital, feeling more uncomfortable and alone than since my early days in the orphanage, my mother came to me in a dream, as she had before, but a dream so true that its dreamlike quality perplexed me.

"Jacob, just as Semmelweis's aqueous solution of chloride and lime sterilized the hands of physicians and ended childbed fever, you will find the solution to end the infections of wounds. But the choice of poisons against bacteria is only the beginning. The work will outlive you as it has outlived me, but you will ignite a glorious eternal process."

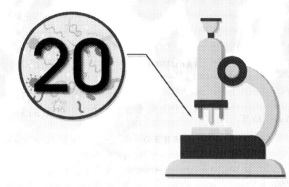

IN THE
SURGICAL
SUITE

U nfortunately, neither Lister nor I was a chemist, and few had
yet turned their attention to how one might destroy bacteria
other than by my heating method.

Semmelweis had used the chloride of lime in his mandatory
hospital sink because it had been shown to get rid of the odors
that were so present in cadaver labs. In the town of Carlisle, near
Edinburgh, carbolic acid had been used to get rid of the odor
emanating from garbage dumps and had been shown to neutralize
the odor of liquid waste used in fertilizer. And so we agreed that
carbolic acid would be the antidote to start with.

I attended my first operation as part of the Lister surgical team,
prepared to use carbolic acid to kill any bacteria in the operative
wound by packing it with a gauze soaked in the acid.

Patient John, age twenty-one, was a worker in an iron factory.
He had been admitted with a fracture of his left leg. He had been

supervising an iron box being raised by a crane. One of the chains slipped, and the five-hundred-pound box fell from a height of four feet upon the inner side of the patient's leg. The patient had collapsed in a mud-soaked field. A bone in his leg, the tibia, was fractured in its middle, and a bloody piece of bone stuck out of the patient's leg. The leg quickly had become very swollen. It had taken several hours to get the patient to the hospital.

In our operating room, Dr. Lister squeezed out clotted blood and fluid from the leg. The wound where the bone had protruded was an inch and a half long and three-quarters of an inch broad. Dr. Lister and his assistant Dr. A. Cameron then made an incision in the wound to acquire cleaner edges. This caused a great deal of additional bleeding.

At this point it became more difficult for me to view the operation as I began experiencing a slight blurring of vision and a feeling that, although it was not possible, it would be beneficial for me to lie down. I also developed some nausea, which I attributed to the excitement of my first surgery and lack of appetite at breakfast. While I had the urge to leave the surgical suite, I knew that my time was coming to take samples for microscopic review and to direct the instillation of carbolic acid into the wound.

"Jacob, you look a bit peely-wally," said one of the surgeons.

"Meaning what?" I asked.

"Meaning pale and sick-looking," he answered.

The last thing I would later remember was an assistant taking from me a piece of lint four inches square, soaked with carbolic acid, to be placed in the wound.

I awoke to find myself a patient in the Glasgow Infirmary. I noted some pain in my jaw and some difficulty in closing my mouth. I felt a hole in my gums where a tooth had been. A nurse was standing above me and applying some ice to my face.

Shortly thereafter, Dr. Lister and Dr. Cameron came by my hospital bed.

"Jacob," said Dr. Cameron with some heavily disguised amusement, "you dislocated your jaw, but fortunately, there was no fracture. We easily put the jaw back in place. So you won't need any carbolic acid." He said the last bit with a sardonic smile.

"But what happened to me?" I asked.

"You fainted, Jacob," said Lister, "probably at the sight of blood. It has happened to many in the past, even medical students and young doctors."

Although I was mortified, I made a commitment to return to the operating room as part of this team. I had come too far to turn back.

"Do I need training to avoid the same happening again?" I asked.

"No," replied Lister. "It is unusual to have a second faint in the operating room. What we first learn, we best know. You must be knackered. Return to your quarters, get some sleep, and be ready for tomorrow."

"Jacob, Dr. Lister continued, what is important is that patient had a boggin' wound, a compound fracture, a bone sticking out of his leg for hours before it could be cleaned and debris and soil removed from it. This wound would develop pus and redness and swelling under usual circumstances. But we have continued to put carbolic acid in the wound and will see what result we get."

My jaw stopped hurting as I realized the war against bacteria had begun.

The next day, I went to visit the patient as I had been trained to do by Lister. "John, how is your leg feeling today?" I asked.

"With the pain medication, it is doing OK, Doctor."

"Well, I am not your doctor, but I am working with Dr. Lister. Let me look."

I took off the tin sheet wrapping. Covering the wound was a piece of gauze or lint that had been soaked in carbolic acid. I added another piece of lint, also soaked in carbolic acid, producing a crust of clot, lint, and carbolic acid. The tin sheet had sufficient firmness to replace the usual splint.

"I will replace your dressing twice per day and add this solution, which will keep your wound healing in a healthy manner. We will measure your leg width every day and keep track of your temperature.

You have a severe injury, but we are going to guarantee that it heals well."

"Thank you, Doctor. When will I be able to walk again?"

"Well, John, I am not a doctor, but I will get you an answer from Dr. Lister."

"Thank you. You seem like a doctor to me."

After several days, Lister examined the wound with me. We wanted to be sure the carbolic acid would not damage the tissue in such a way that it would prevent healing. But he was very satisfied with the healing process.

We continued the carbolic acid treatment for three weeks. After six weeks, the leg had healed as if it had been only a simple fracture. Even Dr. Cameron was surprised. There was no pus, no spreading redness, no foul odor. This was a great victory. I had assisted in the care of a patient, not a wine sample or a silkworm but an exceptionally fine person. I thought, *There is more to being a doctor than what is known or not known. It is an occupation that would fit me.* Yes, I had considered it before. But now it seemed real. How I would have liked to discuss it with my mother or with Adrienne!

I was living in hospital quarters, much like the young trainees. Of course, this was acceptable to me because I had no family or friends in Scotland. But I was surprised that the young surgeons training in Glasgow also had given up many of the joys of the outside world.

These doctors came to treat me well and wanted to learn more about who I was. I even received an invitation to join them at the nearby pub. The Old College Bar on High Street was the place to be for the young and educated in Glasgow. The place had a ceramic-tiled entrance and three rooms: a restaurant, lounge, and bar. The bar was on the second floor and was accessed by a mahogany staircase. There were pictures on all four walls of previous guests, including what looked like many football teams.

We sat around a mahogany circular table: me and Drs. Cameron, Buchanan, and Ebert, all members of the Lister surgical team. Our waitress brought out many bottles of beer and seemed to recognize the group.

These were young men, perhaps only a few years older than I was. One waitress suggested that we did, in fact, look like members of a local sports team. Having had a very successful growth spurt in France and having done much of my moving about by walking, I looked much like an athlete myself.

"So, Jacob, there are so many rumors about you," said Archibald Cameron. "What is your story?"

"Well, I have been a lab assistant."

"For the great Pasteur?" asked Dr. Ebert.

"Yes, I worked with Pasteur for seven years."

"And where did you go to school?" Dr. Buchanan asked.

"I guess I would say in Vienna."

"So are you studying to be a doctor?"

"Perhaps someday. I want to have a career as a scientist and a doctor."

I realized it would be hard to know just what to share with this group, but as we drank more beer, we seemed to be, actually, on the same team.

"You know, Jacob, fainting in the operating room does not exclude you from being a surgeon someday," Dr. Ebert said with kindness.

"Well, I wouldn't want to be doing surgery that resulted in patients dying of infection."

Just as I thought that I had said the wrong thing again, Dr. Ebert saved me by saying, "Nor do we."

"Jacob," said Archibald, "if you can save us from surgeries that go bad, you will be more than just one of us. You will be our *gaisgeach*, our hero!"

The others all agreed. "*Slainte mhath*, let's drink to that", said Dr. Cameron.

I think that is when I realized that I had a role to play in Glasgow. This antisepsis role would be tolerable even over the years it would take to complete. I wished that Pasteur, Adrienne, and the whole group could be with me. But I could live like a surgery trainee, do my cultures, plant our carbol, report the results, and begin the real war against the animalcules—or, as I might now say, bacteria.

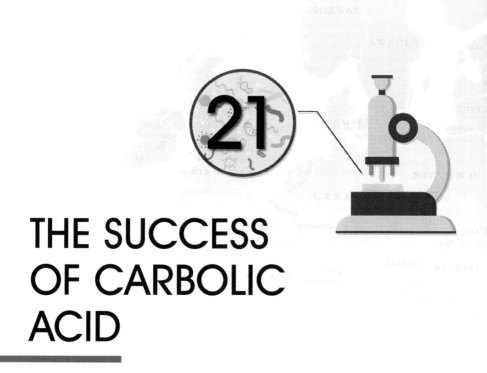

THE SUCCESS OF CARBOLIC ACID

"**J**acob," said Dr. Lister, "we are coming to a critical point where all our surgeries will be treated with and protected by carbolic acid. You have become a critical part of the team, preparing the carbolic acid, taking samples for microscopic investigation, and administering the lint preparation over the wound. We will follow the patients closely to see if the carbol and extra protection from the environment will give us better results. I hope to be reporting our results in cities all over Europe. Jacob, you probably already know that in the past, when we set a fracture in which the bone had eroded through the skin, our results were very poor. Many of our patients had limbs that became filled with pus and later died."

"What a terrible secret to keep from the public, much like the secret of childbed fever," I said with some hesitancy.

"No, Jacob, we have reported our results to the Medico-Chirurgical Society of Glasgow and the British Medical Association.

When we treat complicated fractures in the setting of traumatic events, the prognosis for the patient is poor. That is what we are trying to correct."

"Dr. Lister, I also am confident that the carbol bandage treatments will help, but I think we need to do more."

"And what else do you suggest?"

"That there may be germs in the air. Can we not spray the carbol in the air of the operating room?"

"And you know that will kill the bacteria in the air?"

"It is just my intuition."

"Then it will be done," Lister agreed.

"And one more thing that I almost fear to mention to you. Your team and you yourself do not always wash your hands, and you wear the same clothes in one surgical case after another."

"And what would you suggest?"

"Perhaps to wash your hands after every single surgical case and wear new clothes in case the bacteria of one patient may be transmitted from you to the next patient. At least take off your coat. I appreciate your starched white shirt but roll up your sleeves. Maybe even wear gloves."

"Jacob, you may be mad or just ahead of your time. I have been informed by Mr. Pasteur that you have a special sense of scientific truth, perhaps even an ability to predict the future like no one else has! But we are surgeons first, not scientists or microscopists. Surgeons will not be ready to change how they do things. Our work is challenging enough without having to worry about changing clothes or, heaven forbid, wearing gloves. With that said, I will consider your suggestion."

"Obstetricians have not changed their views either on how to prevent childbed fever," I reminded him. "I don't know that I can always predict the future, but I do know that someday all surgeons will wear gloves in the operating room."

"Mate, we have another case to attend to, a very challenging one. Let's do one day at a time."

I joined the group in the operating suite. An eleven-year-old boy was lying on a table that was covered in white sheets. The boy's head was raised up on a large pillow. The table was perhaps six feet long. There were also two tiny tables and a foot square that held instruments, bandages, splints, and the carbol solution. Dr. Lister and three surgeons surrounded the boy on both sides of the table. I stood back temporarily. The surgeons were dressed in their suits, white shirts, and bowties. A cart had passed over one of this child's limbs, and there was a large wound about an inch and a half long and an inch wide around where the bone was protruding. The surgeons cleaned the wound and trimmed the edges of hanging tissue. I noted the blood on their hands, bloody hands that they seemed to almost enjoy. I stepped closer to the table. My surgical queasiness was gone. I used a cotton swab to sample the bloody wound. I placed the lint soaked in carbolic acid into the wound. Splints padded with cotton wool were placed around the limb. The boy cried and moaned, but there was no need to use chloroform to render him unconscious, although that was an option that the surgeons did have.

Dr. Lister and I visited the young boy every day. We did not remove the splint until day four. The skin was somewhat irritated, but there was no pus. We decided to dilute the carbol with olive oil to prevent skin irritation. The carbol treatment continued for several more days. Afterward, Lister celebrated a wound that had healed without complications.

Of course, to me it was unclear how the outcome might have been different without carbol. I was also a bit frustrated in that I had been unable to find bacteria in the wound either before or after the carbol treatment.

The following day, I was part of an even more challenging case. And I was proud to say that we were ready to aerosolize a carbol solution into the air of the operating room. Ian was a fifty-seven-year-old laborer who had been working in a quarry when a massive stone block weighing six or seven tons fell around and over him. His thigh bone was broken and driven through the skin above the knee. The right collarbone was also fractured. There had been only one companion on the scene at the quarry, so medical attention had been delayed, and in the meantime, John had lost a great deal of blood. He had been brought to the Glasgow Infirmary about six hours after the accident.

Dr. Cameron attended to the patient first as we waited for Dr. Lister's arrival. We removed a shirt strip that had been used to stop the bleeding, which already smelled of death. Dr. Cameron squeezed out blood from the open orifices. Even though the patient seemed deathly ill, and his whole thigh and calf were swollen with blood, I was asked to swab the open wound, and together we introduced carbol lint as a first step, using an instrument that they called a dressing forceps. We sprayed the room with the carbol solution as well.

When Lister arrived, he determined that amputation would be too dangerous because the patient was unconscious and had low blood pressure. So he chose to add more carbol and use pieces of tin to cover the wounds and carbol bandages and then added another bandage around the tin pieces.

The patient improved slowly. On the fifteenth day, a bulge appeared over the fracture. There was pus between the tin and the limb. When I reviewed this material under the microscope, I did see germs, animalcules in great quantities.

While I was not totally satisfied with my view and yearned for a better microscope, a better magnification, the bacteria were clearly visible. This time they looked all the same. There were not sticks and dots and rods, but only clumps of circles, very much grapelike in their clustering. While the carbol perhaps had not killed all the bacteria, it did seem to have kept them in check and kept them from spreading to the rest of the body. Dr. Lister drained the pus easily, and eventually this very sick man went home in good health.

Day after day, I was part of the surgical team. A sixty-two-year-old lady missed her footing and fell down a flight of stairs, breaking her right forearm, with a detached fragment of radius projecting from the wound. Carbolic acid and splints were applied. After several days, there was some redness around the wound but no pus. I saw bacteria again, but while these were also round, they were a bit smaller than those I had seen previously and were grouped together in chains, not in grapelike clusters. She did very well and was discharged after four weeks.

A young boy came to the operating room because he had fallen down the hold of a ship, landing upon his head. He was very confused, constantly asking us who we were and where he was. There was no external wound and no opportunity for carbol treatment. There was tenderness over his sinuses, and his eyeball was protruding. Pus drained from his eye a few days later, and an area of swelling was drained. This time the pus had a foul odor. Under the microscope there appeared to me to be multiple different types of bacteria, although again I yearned for a better view.

I learned from this case that sometimes the bacteria might come from within the patient's own body and not the air or the surgeon's hands.

Each day, there were more cases, difficult cases related to trauma.

I worked and studied with Dr. Lister for three years. We compared his surgical results before the carbol treatments and after. Before the antiseptic period, there had been sixteen deaths in thirty-five cases; after carbol, there were six deaths in forty cases. These results were published in *The Lancet* in 1870. In the journal Lister wrote, "If the history of all contused wounds of hands and feet that have been treated in my wards during the last three years were recorded, it would be enough to convince the most skeptical of the advantages of the antiseptic system."

THE QUEEN

Early one Saturday morning, there was a knock on the door of the tiny hospital room that I called home. I opened the door to find Dr. Lister, who asked me to dress quickly and accompany him to a surgical case that he had been called upon to do in an emergency. It would require traveling to the Scottish Highlands, a destination that I was not familiar with. I grabbed my carbol donkey, a device for spraying carbol into the air that Lister and I had devised.

This would be the first time that Lister and I shared a coach. My life had been one of observing surgeries, which after my first failure I had done with genuine enthusiasm and professionalism; of looking at bacteria under the microscope, which I did with increasing frustration since I was not developing any expertise in interpreting what I knew to be different types of bacteria; and of thinking about Adrienne, whom I had neither contacted nor given up for lost. I had exchanged a few communications with Mr. Pasteur, who had become interested in disease prevention, and there had been the one communication from Neil. I was continuing to think about what Hannah had conveyed to me about life being more than just science.

As we headed to the Scottish Highlands, Dr. Lister told me that he and his wife would be returning to Edinburgh because he had been offered the position of chair of clinical surgery. He would be lecturing and teaching medical students and giving lectures across Europe to defend the germ theory. He would be responsible for multiple operating rooms and for perfecting the carbol system, trying to use waterproof silk, and making other refinements.

"Jacob, you are welcome to come with me. You somehow know the truth about germs, whether it be because of your intuition or your genius, and you will always have a place in my team."

But at that moment, I knew my time with Lister had come to an end. It was not because of my life of limited joy working with him; on the contrary, it was because of my passion to expand the fight against bacteria, a fight that would mean not just surgical antisepsis but also defining diseases and the bacteria that caused them. Although feelings about the value of loyalty had made leaving Pasteur difficult, I had no such concerns about leaving Lister. I had worked hard, almost as hard as his surgical interns, and I had helped him greatly in establishing his reputation as the great surgeon who also cared about bacteria.

"Dr. Lister, I have an interest in better defining bacteria: seeing them better under the microscope, naming them, growing them, proving that they cause specific diseases. May I give you an example?"

He nodded with moderate interest.

"I think that I have seen in your practice different bacteria causing different problems. When you drain an abscess of pure pus, I see spherical bacteria clumping like grapes. When the skin becomes red-hot and spreads across the body, the same spherules seem to be grouped in chains and cause a worse outcome, as they do not form the pus pockets that you can drain. And when the bacteria come from within—from the abdomen or, as with the child with the protruding eye, from the infected sinuses—they have a bad odor, and they look like they are from many different families of bacteria. Can we study these things together?"

"Jacob, I think that you have surpassed my expertise and even what I really feel I need to know. You have helped me keep bacteria out of wounds. And by the way, I have decided to take your advice about hand washing and even wearing gloves, although I am not sure I can sell this to my fellow surgeons.

"In my travels and at international conferences, I have heard that the German government and several German universities may be interested in the kinds of studies, the classification of germs, that you want to do. Perhaps we can find a place for you there. While we find the best colleague for you, you can continue to summarize our final comprehensive experience with carbol."

Just as our conversation was ending, we came upon a palace, the Balmoral Castle. Its huge white walls looked like a fortress protecting a city. It was taller than any building I had ever seen. Cylindrical towers framed the castle, each tower sharply pointing skyward. Its windows were vertically placed so that it was clear that there were at least three floors to the castle. The windows were several feet tall but very narrow. Behind the castle were clear blue skies and green rolling hills. We were greeted by a group of four women wearing long dresses that fell to the floor and fancy multilayered top hats, most of which had colorful flowers. Several men also greeted us, some dressed in dark suits and black top hats, others in more military-looking garb.

"Welcome to the Balmoral Castle, the home of Queen Victoria."

Lister whispered to me, as if he were finally revealing an amusing secret, "Jacob, the queen has an abscess under her arm."

We were guided to the queen's bedroom, where she greeted us in full royal costume, a flowing over-the-shoulder robe, which was white, red, and gold. She wore a large gold necklace and jeweled earrings and a blue-and-silver crown that looked like it had rubies embedded in silver. I noted that she was short, very short—even shorter than Napoleon III—and quite young, perhaps only a decade older than I was. I had no romantic thoughts about her, being as I remained enamored of Adrienne.

I immediately realized the awkwardness of the situation, as she would eventually be as undressed as any other person, rich or poor, who must undergo surgery.

She apparently had been expecting both of us. "Welcome, Dr. Lister and Jacob. Joseph Lister, your reputation as the most accomplished surgeon in Europe is appreciated by the royal family."

"Thank you, Queen Victoria," said Lister. "I have never seen a home anything like this in my life. Wouldn't you agree, Jacob?"

"Perhaps," I said. "But I met Napoleon in the Palace of Versailles. In fact, I stayed in the palace overnight."

Queen Victoria was quite impressed. "So you have met Napoleon? Fine man. I have met him also."

"Yes, I spoke with him when he asked me—well, he asked me and Louis Pasteur—to save the silkworm industry, which we did."

Lister was quite surprised and perhaps embarrassed by my comments, although I did not really understand quite what merited the wild look on his face.

"Well, I am honored to meet both of you," said the queen. "Now, how should we proceed?"

Lister explained to the queen the importance of undressing and finding a sturdy table on which to do the surgery.

Lister, knowing the procedure would not be difficult, had brought a small bag of instruments, and I had brought along the carbol spray and carbol solution. Clearly, it was of great importance to both of us that there be no germ-related complications in this case.

We approached the table on which the now naked queen lay, covered by silk sheets, her head propped up by an elaborate, intricately woven pillow. As Lister set up his instruments, the queen lifted her arm above her head to reveal a large egg-shaped mass. Lister made a small incision in the mass, and pus flowed freely from it, which I took a sample of, as always. I put a small lint of carbol into the incision site and began to spray carbol in the air just as the queen moved her head quickly to see what was being sprayed. This resulted in the spray going directly into her face.

The story of the carbol spray in the face of the queen would be remembered probably for a century to come. Fortunately, my name would not be attached to the story.

As we left the palace and got comfortable in the coach after a successful surgical procedure, Lister turned to me and said, "I am perhaps the only man ever to put a knife to the queen." We were within earshot of our coach driver, so this remark too became part of the legend of the Lister–Queen Victoria visit.

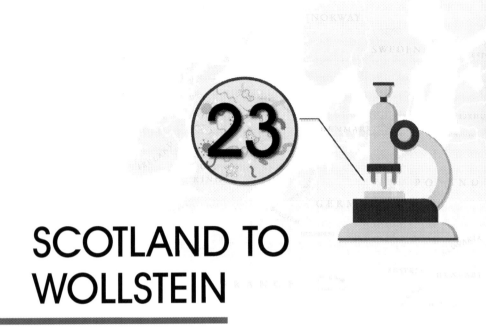

SCOTLAND TO WOLLSTEIN

My meeting with Dr. Lister in 1871 following our visit to the queen would be my last as his assistant, although I would agree to spend some additional time preparing some of Lister's manuscripts as he prepared to leave Glasgow. In this meeting Lister would surprise me with an issue that I had never raised, the monetary value of my work, and then direct me to my next study pathway.

He stood at the doorway of my small hospital room, but he did not appear to be in a rush. I had come to see him as a great surgeon, a kind person, and a man of high standards and ethics. If he had disappointed me, it was only in that my interest in microbes might have been somewhat different from his. As for loyalty, friendship, or commitment to the fine Glasgow hospital—these were not relevant to my decision to move elsewhere. Many physicians and scientists traveled from one opportunity to another frequently.

"Jacob, I want to express my thanks for your work and guidance in helping me establish an antiseptic system that will change how surgery is done forever. I am a man of means, and I am giving you funds that are equivalent to what a young doctor might earn in three years at the Glasgow Infirmary. While you have never needed it and never asked for it, I want to be sure you have the flexibility to continue your scientific career."

"I was born without any resources," I replied with some hesitancy. "I suppose this was as my mother wanted it to be, and I have had little need for material wealth, but I do appreciate your generosity and agree it will make travel and living easier for me."

"I have many contacts around Europe, and I have thought of you as if you were my son or my younger brother pursuing a continued education. Last night I contacted Dr. Rudolf Virchow in Berlin, who is known for his work in investigating typhus. He has studied roundworms and has been interested in the link between animal and human disease. He was no fan of Semmelweis, but he has supported the principles of Pasteur. Unfortunately, he is now more interested in the field of anthropology, and so he was not able to accept you as a student, considering the interests of yours that I described to him. However, he recommended to me a young man just out of the German army who works as a district physician in Prussian Posen. He, like you, is frustrated about how little we know about disease. His wife bought him a microscope, and he is now looking at how to prove that bacteria cause disease. I know that sounds almost humorous, but he is said to be quite extraordinary, perhaps like you, and is likely to make a name for himself. He is only five years older than you are, and he needs some help as long as you can fund your own living conditions, which you are now able to do. His name is Robert Koch.

"I also contacted Dr. Ferdinand Cohn, a professor at the University of Breslau who has known of Koch's work and is willing to use the university's resources to help him. And you will be interested to know that Koch told Professor Cohn that we must improve microscopy to better see the bacteria that might be causing disease. He is frustrated in caring for his patients because we know so little about the diseases that afflict them. He wants to classify different kinds of bacteria. He is a match for you, Jacob, perhaps the best match in Europe."

As I packed my bags, I thought briefly about my father and half brother enjoying the vineyards of Lille; of Neil as a successful medical student in Vienna; of course, of Adrienne; and then of the secondhand advice from nurse Hannah to enjoy life as my mother never had. But I had come this far and would have to agree with this Dr. Koch that aside from the surgical antisepsis, we had learned very little about disease-causing bacteria. I appreciated Dr. Lister arranging my trip to Prussia.

After finishing my scholarly work for Dr. Lister, I said a few brief goodbyes to the surgeons and staff whom I had met. I, like some of the young surgeons, knew that Glasgow was not the final journey. My dreams were not about beautiful homes, restaurants, or vacations. I needed to continue my quest to use science to fight animalcules, bacteria, microbes, or whatever they would come to be called.

Another journey through Europe began, and soon I was on a steamboat from Dover to Calais to cross the English Channel. I was now a paying customer but in tiny quarters, with just a bed and a sink. My door led to a common salon where meals were shared, and passengers congregated.

I left my room to find this common area, which held many circular tables, with ten or so passengers around each table. Most were young men. It was very loud there, with everyone yelling and laughing, and there was a distinct smell of beer. Yes, I had come to appreciate that distinctive smell. In fact, there were puddles of beer on the floor.

Several young men invited me to join them. A few were in military uniform. I drank along with them, recognizing that conversation came easier with beer. After a while, the conversation turned to me.

"What is your name?" asked one traveler.

"My name is Jacob."

"Where are you going, Jacob?" asked another.

"I am going to work with a doctor to study germs that cause illness."

"Germs that cause illness?"

I heard a few chuckles among the group.

"Yes, for example, if you drink sour milk with bacteria in it, it will make you sick. I have done that to prove the point."

As the laughter increased, I realized that had not been the best way to explain my interest.

The conversation moved on without me, and I realized again that there had been a war, a war between France and Prussia, and there were political issues in Europe that were raging but that had eluded my sphere of interest.

"Well, Jacob," said one soldier, "what do you think about this one-year war? Or the news that France has surrendered, and Napoleon III has been captured?"

I thought I saw my way back into this conversation as more and more passengers surrounded our table. "Well, I am friends with Napoleon III, and I helped him save the vineyards and save the silkworms." Perhaps the beer had loosened my tongue.

At this point they raised their beer mugs and toasted my humorous braggadocio. "To Jacob, who has saved the silkworms!"

From another table, a soldier shouted out, "Jacob, and do you know Otto Von Bismarck and Queen Victoria?"

"I do not know Bismarck. However, I do know Queen Victoria and helped remove a lump of pus from under her armpit. She is a fine lady and didn't mind at all when I accidently sprayed her in the face with a bottle of antiseptic."

Now there was more laughter, and I couldn't remember ever being so popular or in such good spirits after multiple mugs of beer. With reflection, however, I realized that often I didn't fit in well with the average group of people. I knew that Adrienne would agree.

I woke up the next morning with a headache and feeling saddened that there had been a war, a war from which I had been insulated and in which many had died for reasons that were unclear. While France and Germany might oppose each other, I remembered the words of Pasteur: "Science knows no country because knowledge belongs to humanity and is the only torch which illuminates the world."

Next, I took my train from Calais to Paris. I knew that Adrienne was still working with Pasteur, now in the Pasteur Institute in Paris, and we agreed to meet.

We met in her new apartment. I had heard that Paris was the most romantic city in the world, but probably not for us. It had been four years since I'd left the Pasteur lab, eleven years since I'd first seen Adrienne, that love-at-first-sight day. I spoke with her in Paris as an adult of twenty-three years. I explained that I was on my way to a small German town to continue to define infectious diseases.

"Jacob, we have so missed you in our laboratory. Louis, he misses you every day. The war has taken a toll on him. His son, Jean Baptiste, has just returned from the fighting in Germany. For a while, he thought his son had died there. He will be disappointed that you have chosen to work with a German."

Adrienne continued, "Drs. Roux and Chamberland now work with us, and Louis has great confidence in them. You will be glad to know that they want to study puerperal fever and to develop vaccines. But Louis has been distracted, is still not well, and fights every day to prove his germ theory to those who will have none of it. I believe his best years may be behind him. You know he still remembers the day in his childhood when a wolf came into town and bit dozens of men, women, and children, giving them rabies. He wants to find the microbe that causes the disease. But he has looked at the saliva of several children with rabies and has never found anything."

"Yes, probably another animalcule too small for us to see."

"Nevertheless, he will try to make a vaccine against it. He remembers your story of how the orphanage children could get measles only once."

"But Adrienne, what about you?"

"I am still an important research assistant for Louis."

"As important as before?"

"Maybe not. No one is indispensable. Jacob, please don't. Surely, you will not ask me to come to a small town in Germany. And I know you will not ask me if I am still in love with you."

"And why not?"

"Well, I will not follow you to Germany for the same reasons I didn't follow you to Scotland."

"Adrienne, this cannot be the last time I will see you."

"Jacob, you tell me. You are the one who Louis says can see the future."

"Well, then we will see each other again."

I left her apartment in the morning.

I found a coach to take me to the tiny town of Wollstein, in Prussia. After an arduous, three-day journey, I would arrive in Wollstein and meet my new colleague, Robert Koch. I had my doubts about this next step. I had worked in a respected Pasteur laboratory and then moved to a busy, academic surgical infirmary. I had worked with a talented laboratory team and with a distinguished surgeon. I had used good microscopes, good surgical equipment.

After spending some nights in several different tiny inns and traveling from city to rural farmlands, I arrived in a town that few people knew and met a man who worked in his home office—studying bacteria, supposedly part-time—while he took care of patients as a country doctor, a man who had received a microscope from his wife for Christmas. But who was I to look down upon or doubt anyone? I had grown up in an orphanage without a formal education, had no real parents, had had one true friend, and had had only one girlfriend, if I might use that term.

The Koch farmhouse was a wooden two-story structure with a long-hipped roof that extended to the ground. It had been built to withstand snowfall and heavy winds. The farmhouse was alive with chickens, and the moos of cows could be heard from the back of the house. Instead of vineyards, there were fields of bundled hay. I was greeted by Dr. Koch and his wife, Emmy. He was wearing a formal black suit with a bowtie and thick glasses that gave him an owl-like appearance. His hair was very black, and he had a receding hairline despite his youth. His wife had brown hair and a full, round face. She wore a bonnet with ribbons and flowers, a scarf, and a gray dress with long sleeves that flowed down to her ankles. She was not the one doing the farmwork. And I was introduced to Gertrude, their three-year-old daughter, who peered at me from behind her mom.

"Jacob," said Dr. Koch, "we have heard of your genius and commitment to the study of microbes. If you want to work hard, wake up before the sun rises each morning, and honor our country with your service, you are in the right place."

"I am definitely here to research and to read and study," I answered.

"I see patients during the day, as many as need to see me. What they tell me about their disease, I use to learn. And Jacob, I read. At night I read about new scientific breakthroughs, which I learned to do from Virchow, my mentor. I don't want to brag about myself, Jacob, but I began reading at age five and have never stopped."

I recalled that in the orphanage I had been told that I had started to read at age four, and while this might have been an opening to find common ground, I refrained from pursuing the matter.

"I have no one helping me at this time but my wife Emmy," said Koch. "However, my work is supported by the university, and I am confident we can make progress together.

"We have an extra bedroom, really the only place around here that makes sense for you to stay. You can work in the lab while I see patients, and I will join you in the late afternoon. After you unpack and get some rest, we will start by discussing our own journeys. But this I already know: we are dedicated to the same cause."

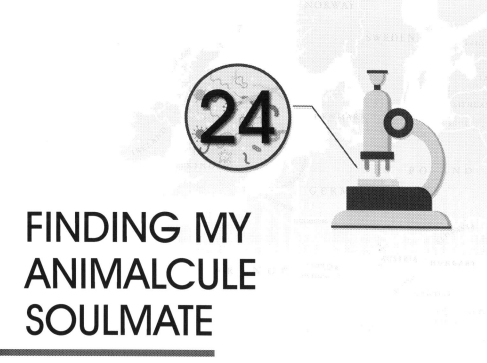

FINDING MY ANIMALCULE SOULMATE

Koch showed me around his home. The living room was heated from a large kitchen. The kitchen housed the important cockle stove, also called the Kunscht. There were bedrooms and guest rooms on the second floor, where I stayed, that were also warmed by the same stove. A cellar of natural stone protected the home from dampness. Through a picture window Koch pointed out several outbuildings just a few hundred yards away, and I did wonder about the opportunity to move into one of them at some point. I was told there was a nearby pond for fishing and a chapel for Sunday services. But most importantly, I was shown a laboratory on the first floor that, as with Pasteur, also served as an office. Another office on the other side of the kitchen was Koch's practice office, from which patients would come and go all day.

The laboratory was surprisingly similar to Pasteur's home laboratory in Alais. Benches were lined up adjacent to two large windows that faced east. There was a desk in the middle of the room, strewn with papers. I was struck by the brightness of the office from both natural light and overhead lighting. The office shelves were lined with more bottles than I had ever seen, and I suspected that they represented both laboratory solutions and patient medications. But my greatest surprise came from a lab accoutrement I had never seen before: wire cages, cages that might be used for the observation of animals.

As I walked to the bench below the windows, I saw the object that would be most important to both of us. It was the Hartnack microscope—a model similar to the microscopes used by Pasteur and Lister—bronze in color, about one foot high, with a monocular lens. There was a stage where a glass slide was secured by a single metal clip, with a mirror below the stage. The scope was lined up with a hole in the stage. There were several different lenses for different magnifications.

Koch sat behind his desk as sunlight reflected off the bronze scope. He was dressed in suit and tie because he was to see patients for most of the day. Everything about him was formal and proper. His foot-long leather doctor's bag was on his desk.

Clearly, the advantage here was the ability to go from the laboratory and microscope to the nearby office where patients with real diseases and problems could be seen and studied all day—not just surgical infections but the diseases caused by animalcules of all kinds. I sat down to speak with Dr. Koch. I was hopeful that he was the man I had been told about—a doctor who would define the diseases caused by germs, who would help define those infectious diseases that caused death and suffering.

"So, Jacob, as someone who has always worked by himself, only with the assistance of my wife, I welcome your presence. And what do you think about the office?" he asked, perhaps wondering if my new surroundings were acceptable.

"Dr. Koch, the office is impressive. Your microscope is similar to the scopes that I have been using. While it gives me confidence to use them, you must know that they are inadequate."

"Well, 'inadequate' would depend on what you hope to use them for."

And so began our conversation about finding germs, a conversation that would last for years, a conversation about what we each hoped to find, what we hoped to accomplish, and what our legacy together might be.

"Tell me, Jacob, what you have accomplished working with Pasteur and Lister, for I am now quite familiar with their work, with your work."

"Doctor, I have seen bacteria everywhere—in wine, in silkworms, on my hands, in sour milk, and in the wounds of very sick patients."

"Yes," said Koch, "I understand that and appreciate Pasteur's identification of germs, of bacteria. And I know that he, with your help, saved the wine industry, saved the silkworm industry. But how did that help doctors like me, who are treating patients with diseases?"

"It did not."

"In fact, you did not even save the sick silkworms—only separated them from those silkworms that were well," he said with authority.

"Dr. Koch, I know that what you are saying is true. And in fact, that is why I moved across Europe to work with Dr. Lister, a real doctor who was treating patients and who recognized that bacteria caused patient deaths. We used carbol and prevented wounds from getting infected."

"Jacob, what bacteria did you see, and what disease did they cause?"

"As you know, I could not see them well enough to categorize them. I believe that they were of different types, but I cannot be sure. I think, perhaps, and I know you can help me here, that there were clumped spherules that caused pus-filled wounds, chaining spherules that caused streaking skin inflammation, and also some very mixed germs, which smelled bad."

"So that is all you have accomplished in your years with Pasteur and Lister?"

"Yes, and that is why I am here with you today. I have made myself and my dead mother a promise to find the bacteria that cause diseases."

"Jacob, I do not want to minimize your accomplishments or your passion, but do you even know what diseases are?"

"I have seen typhus kill children in the Vienna Foundlings. I have seen a leg wound kill a middle-aged man. I was with Pasteur when his daughter died of typhoid fever. I know my mother died of childbed fever. I do have the passion to find and kill the bacteria that cause these diseases."

"Did you ever think that a medical school education might help you understand the diseases that you are up against? Have you shown, with the help of your esteemed colleagues, any particular bacteria that can definitely cause any specific disease?"

"We have not. Pasteur, Lister, and I have not proven that a particular bacterium causes a particular disease, or even that different bacteria are causing their own specific diseases. With respect to medical school, if you will forgive me, I have had little confidence in the doctors I have met, perhaps with the exception of some surgeons, who appear to be in a more technical trade. Doctors do so much, but they do not understand what they are doing or why."

Koch looked at me not at all with anger, but with, I believe, an expression of sadness and regret. It was at that moment that I knew I had finally found my microbe-hunter soulmate.

"Jacob, I too think that those diseases that you mention might well have a particular bacterium causing them.

"There is a disease called anthrax, woolsorter's disease, that is killing our cows and sheep, and people who have been exposed to these animals also have died. In four years, there have been over five hundred deaths in farmers and fifty thousand in livestock. There are some professors at the local university at Breslau who believe they have seen bacteria in the blood of dead sheep. I would like to prove with your help that anthrax is a particular bacterium causing a very serious life-threatening disease.

"Are you willing to do the work needed to address this issue, as you did with the issue of spoiled wine and silkworms?"

"Yes, of course. That is why I am here, sir."

"Together we can understand disease and care for patients—new discoveries for the glory of Germany," Koch declared, speaking loudly with one arm raised, almost in a salute.

"Sir, as Mr. Pasteur would say, science knows no country because knowledge belongs to the world and is the torch that illuminates humanity."

Koch grimaced. "Is not Pasteur a French patriot?"

"Yes, he is a man who loves his country."

"My friend, you do realize that I have returned from a war with France, a war in which many soldiers died?"

"Yes, but for what? What was the reason for the war?"

"Complicated, but it had mostly to do with the leadership of Spain," he said hesitantly.

"It is a bad omen that powerful neighbors like Germany and France have developed a hatred over issues that are hard to understand, complicated issues. And I see many more deaths in the future."

"Jacob, you can tell the future of Europe as well as find the animalcules?" Koch said with sarcasm.

"I have been told that at times I can predict the future."

"Jacob, I am a soldier. I am just back from the war. I put myself in danger. I had to fight back the fear of dying each day. In working with me, you won't be dealing with wine or silkworms. Have you really been there and watched as someone died from a disease?"

"Yes, I have."

"And that does not frighten you?"

"Probably no more than it frightens you, sir."

"Well then, we will start work tomorrow."

"We will be using science to help all mankind," I said with confidence.

Koch shrugged his shoulders, unwilling to debate further.

This small German town was my destiny. Perhaps God, my mom, or fate had put me in the very best place.

ANTHRAX

Emmy and I traveled by horse and buggy to the surrounding farms in the area. I would ask for sheep that were sick or that had recently died. We had no difficulty finding them, as this woolsorter's disease appeared to be everywhere.

But there was a learning curve to this effort of drawing blood from a dying sheep. First of all, I was surrounded by sheep that were well and even by onlooking family members of the poor afflicted sheep. Anthrax death often came swiftly, and my first patient looked at me with fear and suspicion. He was a large fellow, at least from what I perceived to be sheep size, and was already somewhat bloated, confused, and bleeding from the mouth. Emmy showed me how to hold the animal, whose wool coat was covered with dirt. The sheep held still but urinated and defecated in fear. It was not difficult to locate a vein in the neck. The needle penetrated the vein, and blood was collected in a glass tube. We repeated the process as we found more sick sheep. And I knew there might be anthrax-stricken cows and horses in my future as well. But I reminded myself that I was learning about anthrax so as to prevent human suffering from the disease and perhaps to help these pathetic animals as well.

Bringing those samples back to the laboratory, I again spent many days peering through the microscope, one eye closed, hoping that the light would be adequate, separating extraneous dirt and fiber from what I needed to see: deadly microbes. The lighting was better than I had been used to in the Lister laboratory, and the water immersion lenses gave us a better view of the bacteria. There was no doubt that bacteria, bigger than I was used to seeing and more rodlike, existed in the blood of the very sick sheep.

In the evening, after finishing his work with his patients, Dr. Koch would view the bacteria with me.

"We need the blood of healthy sheep as well, Jacob. And we need better visualization. Some of the bacteria seem to be elongating, and some have little spherules on them. I will speak with Hartnack myself to see how the visualization can be improved."

I continued to study the blood of sick sheep and cows as well. I also obtained samples from healthy sheep and cows. There were almost always rods in the blood samples of the sick animals but never in those of the healthy ones. We also heard from farmers that anthrax might disappear for months and then return without any new animals being introduced to the farm. We all wondered where the anthrax might be hiding and in what form, but that was a question for another day.

To further our investigations, we spent weeks looking at other tissues of dead animals. Cutting open a dead animal in the field became routine, but my first case gave me a feeling similar to my first case in Lister's operating room. Finding the spleen, an organ that had seemed to collect large numbers of bacteria, was easy after some brief preparation with an anatomy book. We found rods in the lymph nodes and especially the spleens of dead animals.

I had considered looking in on some of Dr. Koch's patients but in fact had little time at my disposal during the day beyond my laboratory work. But one evening Dr. Koch asked me to accompany him to see a very ill patient on a nearby farm.

Jonathan was a wool sorter who had been complaining of fever, sore throat, neck swelling, and hoarseness. In the past few days, he had developed a cough and shortness of breath. There was a large skin ulcer on his arm that he said had developed from a cut on his arm that he'd received while collecting wool.

Dr. Koch sat at his bedside and listened to his story. He noted the patient's pulse and rate of respiration and examined him thoroughly, carefully looking at his skin, listening to his heart and lungs with a stethoscope, feeling for the size of his liver and spleen, and checking him for neurologic function.

"Jonathan," said Dr. Koch, "I believe that you have anthrax, and you probably caught it while tending to a sick sheep. It appears to be at a late stage, but I will visit you each day and can give you some medicine for any pain you may have, and perhaps I can improve your breathing. We will be taking some blood from you and a sample of what you are coughing up."

When we returned to the laboratory that night, we looked at Jonathan's samples and found the same rods in his blood and sputum that we had seen in sick farm animals. These bacteria were large and present in great numbers. They sometimes seemed to be elongating, as we had seen before. Absent were the round bacteria in clumps or chains that had appeared in some wounds of the Lister patients.

We returned to see Jonathan each night. Dr. Koch applied cold compresses to his forehead and gave small amounts of opium for pain and camphor for the skin lesion. He asked Jonathan's wife to boil some water for tea.

Jonathan's symptoms worsened each day, and Dr. Koch got the family together to speak with them. "Jonathan will die of anthrax," he told them. "We have no treatment, and his time on this earth will be short."

The family was very appreciative of everything that Dr. Koch had done. But I was not at all impressed. The night that Jonathan died, and we returned to the office, I had to express my dissatisfaction.

"You asked me why I have not gone to medical school. This case is why. You have no understanding of his disease and no treatment, only words and potions, unproven."

"Jacob, you do not seem to know what we do as physicians. We cannot cure most diseases, although we can adequately treat some. We are always learning more about disease as the years go on, and that will never change. We help patients to cope, we relieve pain, we explain that which we understand. In fact, we can almost always offer something to make the patient's journey easier even if death is the final outcome. If that is not enough for you, then you are right—stay a scientist and never become a doctor."

I thought of Paul, whom I'd watched over until his death, cooled off with river water, and kept company till the end. I remembered the children whom I had attended even to death from typhus. I hoped that someone had been there to comfort my mother at the very end when there was no understanding or treatment for childbed fever. And at that moment I understood. I pledged to myself that when my scientific work was done, I would find myself a school of medicine. And I resolved that someday we must find a treatment for disease caused by deadly animalcules.

THE NEW ERA
OF INFECTIOUS
DISEASES

Koch finished seeing his patients, and we met in the laboratory to review microscopic samples and plan for our ongoing work. Koch was filled with enthusiasm that we had made a major scientific breakthrough by showing that the microbes, which consistently looked the same, as rod-shaped germs, were always seen in sick animals but never in healthy ones.

"Dr. Koch, I agree, but I do not think that this is proof that these rods are causing the disease. They might be the consequence of a different process."

"I know you are just testing me," said Koch. "But what further evidence would you like to see?" Koch looked at me as if to challenge my very existence.

"We could take a sample of rod-filled blood, put it on a splinter of wood, and inject it into me. If I became ill, that would be proof that bacteria cause disease."

Koch did not know whether to be amused or frightened by my simple suggestion.

"I once drank some spoiled milk and did get sick. That action confirmed to me that the germs in the milk caused disease."

"Jacob, that suggestion reflects poorly on you, but that discussion is for another day. We need an animal model—perhaps one of Gertrude's pets; she has both a rabbit and a guinea pig."

I had been thinking about the importance of getting on well with Gertrude if I was to continue living in the same house and so quickly rejected that idea.

But Koch solved the problem by saying, "There are pesky white mice in our barn. They can become an animal model for disease."

"A brilliant idea! Perhaps white mice will become a model for others in the future as well. Yes, I can see that."

"Jacob, tomorrow I will leave it up to you and Emmy to gather the needed mice. Perhaps Gertrude could help as well, although there will be no need to explain our project in any detail."

Emmy and I started our day in the barn. While there were mousetraps available, we needed the mice well, unaffected by trauma to the tail. We descended upon the barn with large glass jars and small bits of cheese and meat. Some mice were quite accommodating, whereas others had to chased around the barn. It was a great activity for me, Gertrude, and Emmy to get to know each other. By the end of the day, we had twelve white mice, one in each large jar with a metal lid, with holes poked in the lid for air. Gertrude decorated each jar with grass, flowers, hay, and soil.

The next evening, I met with Koch to plan an experiment that I had thought about in my dreams for years. This was the experiment that the world needed. We kept two mice untouched (I wanted to make sure that the mice would not die just from being held captive in a glass jar). I prepared sharpened slivers of wood soaked in the blood of sheep who were sick with anthrax, blood that we had confirmed by microscopy was filled with microbes.

I used the first two mice to practice the technique of injecting into the tail vein.

I then injected four mice through the tail vein with blood taken from sick sheep, blood that had been shown to have microbes, rods, in the blood samples. I injected the four remaining mice with blood from healthy sheep, blood that did not have visible rods in the blood sample. We had used a wooden box about the size of a mouse with a hole in it to pull out the tail of each animal. I felt fairly confident that I had entered the tails adequately, having felt a pop as the vein was entered each time.

We would observe the mice each day, measuring their breathing rate and other parameters such as activity and visible changes.

The morning after my evening experiment, without looking at the labels that we had included to describe each intervention, we found four mice who were breathing rapidly and looking ill.

On the second morning of our experiment, four mice were dead—all had been injected with blood from sick sheep. All the other mice appeared totally normal, including the four mice that had been injected with blood from healthy sheep.

I dissected the spleens of the dead mice, and under the microscope, all were filled with the same rods we had seen in the sheep blood.

Koch recognized the importance of the experimental findings, and he called Dr. Cohn at the University of Breslau with our results. He realized that there was much to do before this would be believed and understood. We would need to be able to take pictures, photomicrographs of the rods in the sheep blood. We would need to find a way to stain the bacteria, so we had something to show a journal. Koch had never been adequately respected as a scientist, so he realized there was a long way to go to prove what had been done.

But for me, the experiment was an affirmation of all my life's work, from the time it had been suggested to me that my mother had died of something on the hands of physicians to the years with Pasteur to prove that bacteria even existed. On this day, after my mentorship by Pasteur, Lister, and even Semmelweis, Robert Koch and I had proven that bacteria caused disease. But this was not about just some nonspecific germ that made people sick, not about just bacteria of some sort getting into wounds. Today was the birth of the principle that different bacteria caused different specific diseases, infectious diseases—that there were diseases that spread from one person to another.

There was a microbe, an animalcule, that caused a lethal disease called anthrax. There were likely other germs that caused other diseases. Each would need to be identified and someday cured— perhaps by something like Lister's antiseptic. I believed we had entered a new era, the era of infectious disease.

I was not someone who had learned much about celebration. At dinner, I let the Koch family know that it had been an important day for me, a great day. But I really just wanted to be with Adrienne. I was becoming more of a normal man than just what they called a savant.

POTATOES, CAMERAS, AND A SPECIAL VISIT

Robert was now splitting his time between his practice and the laboratory. We were modifying and repeating our anthrax experiments and reporting results to the university professors who would visit on occasion. Emmy was very much a part of the research team. But Robert and I remained frustrated that we could not better identify differences in the microbes we were seeing in various animal tissues and fluid specimens.

Meanwhile, I had become a member of the Koch family, and we always ate the evening meal together in their kitchen. Around the dinner table, Emmy would ask about my plans in life.

"Jacob, surely you would like a family of your own someday."

These were the conversations that I found difficult. I assumed people saw me as different, and I was indeed different from most, and with good reason.

"Yes, perhaps I will consider that when my work is done, my work with the microbes. I've never had a family life, so it is nothing that I have missed." I was not about to discuss my real reason for being a hopelessly single. "It has been a joy to watch Gertrude grow up and to appreciate what family life means," I said diplomatically, adding, "Gertrude, it has been fun finding mice together."

"Yes, Uncle Jacob, and taking care of my rabbits and chickens. Why don't you have a beard like Daddy, Uncle Jacob, and why do you always just wear a plain white shirt?"

"I don't see patients like your daddy does, and I like to shave in the morning."

"And why do you always wash your hands, Uncle Jacob?"

"We all need to wash our hands to make sure we don't have any germs on them."

"What are germs, Uncle Jacob?"

"Well, germs are like little animals on your hands, but you can't see them."

"Oh, that's funny, Uncle Jacob. Like little chickens that you can't see are playing on your hands!"

"And I have a question for you, Gertrude. Why do you not eat your potatoes?"

"I like to save my potatoes for the guinea pig. I sometimes bring them back to my room and save them there."

"Well, Gertrude, I am not sure that is a good idea. You know, these little animals can be everywhere."

The next morning, Dr. Koch asked me to join him in his office, where he was to see a patient with a leg wound. The man had fallen on a sharp rock a week before, and his leg was swollen and very red. There was a clear fluid draining from the wound but little pus and no pus-filled abscess. I used some carbolic acid on the wound, and I collected the specimen for microscopy.

Later that night, back in the laboratory, I showed the slide of the wound material to Dr. Koch. As I'd suspected based on my experience with Dr. Lister, there were bacteria present, but these were very different from the rods of anthrax. These were the round bacteria that formed chains, sometimes a chain of as many as twenty small round bacteria.

Koch agreed.

But we were disadvantaged in our work. We were not seeing our bacteria clearly enough. And because these bacteria were seen by only one person at a time, they were even perhaps described somewhat differently. There was no record, no good science.

"Jacob, I have drawn the rods and described them as best as can be done."

"But it won't be enough to convince the world that there are different bacteria causing different diseases."

"I learned some photography from my Uncle Edward, as a child," Koch remembered with a smile. "It should be possible to photograph these bacteria."

We knew that we needed help to move forward, and that the science of microscopy was improving. Hence, Dr. Koch composed a letter to Seibert and Kraft of Wetzlar, the leading microscope company in Europe.

He wrote to them, "I have encountered great difficulty in executing proper drawings of bacteria and hope to use photo microscopy to get around these problems. I need an apparatus that is suitable for my work. I need an apparatus that provides the highest magnification, at least twelve thousand. I would be exceedingly grateful if you could inform me as to whether it would be possible to obtain good photographs of tiny transparent objects such as bacteria and if you could advise me which apparatus would be the best for this purpose."

Koch waited impatiently for a response, sending several follow-up letters. The apparatus did arrive within weeks. At first the equipment was unsatisfactory, and Koch and Seibert and Kraft had multiple communications. Eventually, Dr. Koch—by himself, as this photomicrograph endeavor was beyond my imagination or expertise—made taking pictures of germs a reality. It was a horizontal microscope-camera setup. The camera, microscope, and mirror lighting arrangement were aligned on a bench. Sunlight was directed into the microscope with a heliostat, as it was called. Pictures were taken on an emulsion-coated glass plate. Robert was never quite satisfied with our bacteria pictures, and while I continued to work to obtain and categorize specimens, he communicated with many others who also were interested in photomicroscopy for various scientific reasons.

I still remember the day that Dr. Koch called me to the laboratory late one evening. I had never seen him express such joy and excitement; it was like he was experiencing multiple Christmas days from his childhood all at once. He had been working with a package from Seibert, after again asking for the latest technology to push the science of microscopy. An oil immersion lens had arrived, along with an oil that would be placed between the bacteria specimen and the new lens. We could now see bacteria magnified by more than a thousand times their original size.

Several months later, when I was hunting for mice with Gertrude, she had more questions for me about germs.

"Are they really everywhere, Uncle Jacob?"

"I believe they are. Sometimes they stay to themselves, but sometimes they make people sick."

"And can they really be on a potato?"

"I suppose they can."

"Well, I think so too," said Gertrude. "I think they are growing on my potatoes."

When we returned to the house, Gertrude presented to me her sliced-in-half potatoes, those that she had chosen not to eat at dinner but to save for her pets. The potatoes had tiny round elevations on them. The spots were of several different colors, some clear, others violet, brown, or golden.

I called for Robert to meet me by the microscope.

I grabbed a thin wire. I sampled the material from a golden-colored spot on the potato, mixed it with water, and placed it on the slide. I found round clumps of bacteria, reminding me of the pus-filled wounds that Lister had seen. Another spot on the potato had only rods; a third had corkscrew-like forms. These spots were what I now called colonies.

Gertrude had grown separate colonies of bacteria on her potato. We had created another new world of study. We could grow bacteria on solid material.

As the years went on, Koch's findings gained recognition as our colleagues from the University of Breslau published the proof that anthrax was a bacterial disease. Koch was becoming recognized for a new field of microbiology, a new field of infectious diseases, a field where bacteria could be not only seen under a microscope but also photographed and grown.

THE DREAM

Falling asleep in my tiny room in a small Prussian farm town, I reflected on my successes but questioned myself about who I was and where I was going—what would be my fate? Sometimes, I saw my battle against the microbes resulting in revenge against me by one possibly yet-to-be-determined creature.

But on this night, instead of having the nightmare of an attacking microbe, I found myself in a deathly quiet hospital room with white walls, a white cement floor, and the smell of carbol—Lister's operating room. I was in a white coat, Koch's stethoscope in my pocket, standing over one bed, the only bed in the large hospital room. But I could see bacteria in the air, cocci in long chains. In the hospital bed, looking angelic, with equally white skin, was my mother. While I had imagined her before, I did realize that I had never seen what she looked like and never really had asked anyone, like my father or Semmelweis, who would know. I always preferred to see her, hear her, touch her hand as my mind would choose in my dreams.

"Mother, I have changed the course of history, I believe, by proving that germs killed you and so many others—germs that I think have caused childbed fever, anthrax, typhus, wounds, and perhaps things that have not yet even been discovered."

"You have accomplished so much with so little. But you are living life as I did, without joy."

"Joy seems so unimportant in the hunt for microbes."

"But why are you in your battle other than to enable others to live and enjoy their lives? Are you making the same mistake that I made in life? For me, it was studying, medical school, obstetrics training, years of sacrifice and service, fighting for the truth, without fulfillment."

"What would you have me do?"

"Have you known joy at all in all your now twenty-six years?"

"I could better describe the last microbe I saw than describe what joy I have seen. But I might say sometime in Lille, sometime in the country with my half brother and father, and in all my moments or hours with Adrienne."

"Well, perhaps your father is one to teach you how to enjoy life, as that is what he is known for. But as for Adrienne—why are you not with her?"

"She rejected me, and I have accepted that."

"But you survived the orphanage without giving up, found your way to France on your own, moved across the English Channel and back. For a fighter, you have given up on Adrienne quickly."

"Well, no one has ever suggested that to me."

"Perhaps you need to find her and also reunite with your father. He is, for all his faults, your father and a man who knows how to teach you to enjoy life. What else do you want to accomplish, Jacob?"

"I want to find the bacterium that causes childbed fever and convince the world—Budapest, Vienna, London, Paris—that it is a bacterium that has caused so many women to die."

"And have you found that bacterium?"

"I am not sure, but I suspect it is the cocci in chains, the one that forms necklaces and may come to be called streptococci, as 'necklace-like' in Greek."

"And what else do you hope for yourself?"

"To be a doctor, but a good doctor—one who has the skills of Lister and the compassion of Koch, the wisdom and knowledge of Pasteur, and the commitment that they told me you had to your patients."

"That will require starting from the beginning in medical school, won't it?"

"I suppose that it will."

"And where would you go? Vienna? Paris? Edinburgh?"

"I don't know. I don't like the wars here. The Franco-Prussian War has left hatred and division. I have even heard of dislike between Koch and Pasteur. Many don't like Austrians. I believe things in Europe may only get much worse. So perhaps I will study to be a doctor in America. Their war is over. Perhaps it could be a new start for me."

"And their studies on microbes?"

"There is a new school that wants to correctly teach what I have discovered."

"And that is what you aspire to do?"

"No, there is one more challenge that I will meet—to find the treatment for all the diseases caused by the microbes."

"And how will you know how to do that?"

"By finding ways to kill bacteria, like with Lister."

"But you want to kill bacteria that are already in the body of a person?"

"Yes, that would be the plan."

"You would have to know about drugs and blood and disease beyond your reach, beyond current scientific knowledge."

"Well, perhaps a man's reach should exceed his grasp."

"Jacob, the treatments, the cures for microbe-caused diseases, will be beyond your life years. Do not plan for the impossible. It is a way to make yourself truly unhappy."

Then my guiding light faded in the night. I was alone again, on my own but with a plan.

CONSUMPTION

I had been ready to move from Wollstein and chart a new course for my life. I had moved into a converted barn as a home for me, but with Gertrude growing up, it did seem more and more awkward to always be around the family, even though I clearly had been adopted as Uncle Jacob, and my role in the laboratory was critical. Koch had added an assistant, a Dr. Gaffky, who was rapidly learning the laboratory skills.

Koch and I together had proven that particular bacteria cause specific diseases, using anthrax as a definitive model. Koch had improved his photomicroscopy and begun taking pictures of any and all bacteria. And thanks to Gertrude, we had been able to grow bacteria on the pure culture of a potato half, improving the methodology using gelatin or beef broth.

But just before I was to leave, a patient who would change my plans came into Koch's office. Felix was a thirty-six-year-old laborer who worked in building construction. He had been healthy all his life, but two months prior to his visit to Dr. Koch, he had begun to cough and lose weight. Dr. Koch, recognizing the importance of this patient's visit at this time, asked me to be part of his interview with the patient.

"At first it was just a cough, nothing that even stopped me from working. Then the cough got worse, and I started to feel feverish at night," said Felix.

"How would you describe the material you coughed up?" asked Dr. Koch.

"Greenish, then with some bloody streaks in it."

"And has the blood in your sputum continued or gotten worse?"

"Yes, sometimes it is quite bloody."

"Have you had any sweats at night?"

"Yes, I am always sweating at night."

"Do you wet your bedclothes with sweat at night?"

"Yes, often my shirt is drenched at night and the bedsheets as well."

"And how much weight have you lost?"

"I was a hundred and eighty pounds, and now I am a hundred and fifty."

"And that has been over two months?"

"Yes."

"Is there anyone else at your work who is sick?"

"There are two or three others who are coughing, men I work very closely with—similar complaints, bringing up blood."

Koch arranged for the hospitalization of the patient. It was hoped that rest and a special diet would help, but the prognosis was poor.

After the patient left the office, Koch spoke to me with an urgency in his voice. "Phthisis, the white plague, tuberculosis. It has been known since the times of ancient Egypt, but its cause is unknown. It has been postulated to be caused by bad air, by vampires, by a curse of the gods. Hippocrates called it the disease of dry seasons."

"I am familiar with this disease. I saw the bloody cough, the spread among children, the weight loss and death in the orphanage."

"And you know why I wanted you to see this patient?"

"Yes, Robert, you wanted me to see this patient because the phthisis is caused by a microbe?"

"Of that, there is no doubt."

"Dr. Koch, the disease is slowly progressive. I doubt you would find the microbe in the blood."

"No, we shall look for it in the bloody cough material."

We planned to follow the patient in the hospital and obtain material from when he coughed or even from his sweat at night. However, the unfortunate death of the patient within the week gave us a new opportunity.

Koch brought me with him to perform Felix's autopsy. As had been described by others, the lungs were peppered with numerous yellowish spots. The upper lungs were destroyed, with large cavities replacing normal lung tissue. The liver had similar spots, and the bone marrow tissue had been replaced with scar tissue.

"Jacob, as I did years ago, I will ask you again. I know you have great intelligence, and I have seen you mature over the years. But I want you to assure me again that you are aware that our work can be dangerous."

"Yes, sir. I know that tuberculosis likely goes from one person to another and can cause fever and breathing problems and death. I want to live, but I am with you in this army and in this fight against the microbes."

And then a strange emotion overwhelmed me. I shocked Dr. Koch when I bent over to reach him at his desk and hug him and thank him for caring about me. I realized that I was beginning to change. Wanting to hug someone or be hugged had never been in my nature, and in fact, I was amused by those who were constantly hugging each other.

While we would not have known how to proceed a few years ago, the pathway now was clear. Koch obtained material from the affected lung and spread it on glass slides.

What we saw were tiny, very thin, beaded organisms, not at all like the thick rods of anthrax. They bunched together in lung tissue. Koch's immersion lens made the visualization possible. They could be seen in multiple tissues of the body, the liver and bone marrow especially. Koch had begun to experiment with various dyes in preparation for his photomicrographs. An aniline dye stained the organisms blue.

"This beginning of dyeing the microbes for better visualization will be a pastime for many," I suggested. "Imagine some bacteria staining one color and another bacteria a different color. What a great pastime staining will become!"

In a small laboratory, in a small town in Germany, a country doctor and a Viennese orphan were seeing the culprit, the microbe, the animalcule, that had caused a terrifyingly chronic disease for centuries, now for the first time!

It was time to collect white mice again. However, the stakes were so high now, in this study of one of the worst diseases in human history, that we worked with the University of Breslau to obtain rabbits and guinea pigs. Koch added chickens and even some pigeons. A barn became a menagerie of cages. Never had I worked more eighteen-hour days, spurred by the enthusiasm of Koch, who as a doctor recognized our momentous opportunity.

It took longer than perhaps we would have guessed, but the guinea pigs after some weeks became listless, started shaking, lost their fur, lost their body mass, and died, not one surviving the inoculations given them.

Dissecting the dead animals yielded no surprises—the same slender germs everywhere, the tissues of the animals' bodies looking very abnormal, mimicking the pathologic findings in humans.

We proceeded to study normal sacrificed animals of all kinds, but never could we find these bacteria.

But Koch would not stop. He continued to ask surrounding hospitals to find patients who had died of what I chose to call tuberculosis, a term first coined by Johann Schonlein, a physician in Zurich, who we were told had studied this disease. Koch found numerous autopsy specimens that we proceeded to examine by microscopy and then photograph. We, with most of the work burden falling on myself and Gaffky, continued to amass much more proof than necessary that we had found a microbe that caused tuberculosis. For the first time in my life, I became fatigued, wondering if we might all die of this disease after the hundreds of specimens that we had handled, tired in fact of watching the poor guinea pigs become the sacrificial lambs for our justifiable and great cause.

It was 1881, and I was thirty-three years old. The quest to define the microbe causing tuberculosis was a long, exhausting journey. I was not unaware that I had been part of the great discoveries of my time and perhaps had been responsible for most of them. I was done.

Koch's findings were gaining recognition as our colleagues from the University of Breslau published the proof that anthrax was a bacterial disease. Koch had spun a new field of microbiology.

One morning Koch called me into his office with a letter to show me. "Jacob, imagine a letter from as far away as Norway, from a doctor, Gerhard-Henrik Armauer Hansen. He has seen an organism very much like what we have described in tuberculosis but in a different disease completely. Years ago, he was asked by a group of lepers, actually from your Vienna area, to consider their leprosy as a disease caused by animalcules. The bacteria in their sores evidently looked almost identical to those in the lungs of our tuberculosis patients."

"Must have been Basil and Laslo," I whispered to myself. I wondered if a cure would be far behind.

We had few visitors to the Koch home, but memorable was the visit sometime around 1882 by a William Henry Welch, an American physician. Welch was trained in German pathology and had established a pathology laboratory in Bellevue Medical School in New York City. He had just been appointed to become the future dean of a new medical school that was being planned in Baltimore, the Johns Hopkins Hospital and School of Medicine.

I was present when Koch met with Welch in the laboratory.

"Dr. Welch, it is an honor to have you come to my home, my laboratory, for this visit. And I would like to introduce Jacob, a laboratory assistant who has worked with me for a decade and with both Pasteur and Lister in the past."

Dr. Welch was a large, confident man, with a thin brown mustache and tiny goatee. I appreciated that he looked at us both before speaking.

"Robert, your work is becoming well known around Germany, and soon I suspect it will be known around the world as well." As he spoke, he smiled and seemed very jolly about his opportunity to speak with Koch. He was the type of man who would seem jolly about speaking with anyone, I guessed. "As the dean of what I hope will become the premier medical school in the United States, the very best, I want to be sure I understand the basic premises of your new field of bacteriology and your scientific methodology. Imagine the opportunity to teach those principles to the best and brightest students that we can find."

Koch, recognizing that his words might well become the dogma for future American medical students, chose his reply carefully, his serious nature contrasting with the exuberant Welch's.

"William, these are the principles upon which we have established our science of microbes, or as Jacob might say, the world of animalcules. As with anthrax, the microbe must be found in diseased individuals but not in healthy ones. Inoculation of the microbe in an animal model must produce the disease in that animal, as we have shown for anthrax. And then the microbe should be isolated from the animal or human and shown to be the same as that inoculated."

I could not help but add my suggestions. "Dr. Welch, having worked for Louis Pasteur, I would add that our air contains living organisms that can cause disease under certain conditions. We can kill them by heating them. They can be identified by microscopy, and we are beginning to see that they can be grown on different media—potatoes or gelatins. These bacteria reproduce; they are not born out of soil or water or even excrement."

At this point we showed Dr. Welch dried samples of stained bacteria, our potato cultures, and pathologic specimens, with which he expressed some familiarity.

Dr. Welch asked us many different questions, probing questions that were difficult to answer. How could we be sure that all infectious disease could be reproduced by inoculation or that some animals might not be resistant to diseases that occur in man? And would there not be infectious diseases that, to prove, would require inoculation into human volunteers, which could be very dangerous? And if bacteria were all around us, why were we not always getting sick? And were there perhaps bacteria with a useful purpose? Might there be some patients, and he knew of some with disorders of the blood, who could get sick from a bacterial strain that a well person would not get sick from?

These questions left us with a great deal of humility and recognition of the need to explore our work further.

"Dr. Koch, Jacob, I want to thank you for sharing your knowledge and discoveries with me. I feel the enormous burden to teach my future medical students the truth about infectious diseases. This will be my calling."

"Dr. Welch, will you also inspire your students to not only recognize each infectious disease but also to find ways of killing these bacteria?" I asked.

"Yes, an excellent point. To teach the work of Lister and antiseptics," he said with voice raised and hands to the sky.

"But Dr. Welch, I also mean to kill them while they are in the body of the patient."

"Yes, Jacob, an impressive accomplishment that would be. I surely hope to see that in my lifetime."

"And Dr. Welch, how does one become the dean of a medical school, and why would you travel to see us now?"

"Jacob, although I was born into a family of three generations of physicians, I did not think that medical school was for me. I graduated from Yale and then entered the Sheffield Scientific School. Eventually, I realized that my compassion for helping others was a better fit for medical school. Columbia was a typical American medical school with relatively little clinical training, and so I was advised to come to Germany, where some of the best pathologists and clinicians were working. I studied in Strasburg with Carl Waldeyer, in Leipzig with Dr. Ludwig, and right next door in Breslau. I was ready to travel anywhere to learn about medical education. I suspect that you feel the same. I returned to the United States to develop a science and education laboratory in Bellevue, and its success gave me a reputation as a physician and educator. It was Dr. Cohnheim of Breslau who told me of Dr. Koch's important breakthroughs."

"Dr. Welch, I am a self-made scientist, having had the opportunity to work with Pasteur, Koch, and Lister. But now I am also considering becoming a doctor."

"Well, Jacob, if you decide to do so, you could jump right into an American medical school. You could help me teach the basic principles of bacteriology, and I would welcome you whenever you make that decision."

"But the Johns Hopkins School is not yet in existence."

"It is not, but there are others. I would recommend to you the Boston University School of Medicine, which is of interest because it has just accepted women as medical students, the first time an American medical school has done so."

"I definitely approve of that as my mother was the first female obstetrician in Vienna. She died of childbed fever."

"That is very sad, a disease that in America, Oliver Wendell Holmes has studied."

"Yes, Dr. Welch, it is a disease in which I have a lifelong interest and special knowledge—but that would be for another time. You were recommending schools of medicine in the United States."

"My recommendation would be the University of Pennsylvania, where a young physician from Canada is making a name for himself as one of the great clinicians and teachers in the country. I know you would like to work with him—Dr. William Osler. Sometimes I think Osler's enthusiasm puts me to shame."

Dr. Welch appeared to be a doctor who was interested in science, yes, but mostly interested in understanding the work of others. I knew that he would want to teach his students truth from fiction, without any political biases. He not only could inspire students to pursue what was true but also could guide them in developing new knowledge.

I was prepared to move on with my life, propose to Adrienne, go to medical school, vacation in the vineyards of Lille, ask my father about the joys of life.

But it was not to be—for the greatest challenge of all lay ahead. Who would have predicted a challenge that both France and Germany, political enemies, would be called upon to immediately work on as partners, a challenge that would bring the Koch team and the Pasteur team together? These two teams would need to combat one of the greatest microbe challenges ever.

EGYPT

Asiatic cholera had been plaguing India, wreaking havoc and causing thousands of deaths in poor, crowded communities. But now the disease was being recognized in Egypt, particularly in the city of Alexandria. Alexandria, on the southern coast of the Mediterranean, was an important port of trade, with close connections to the European continent. Although the British had occupied Egypt, they were not as concerned about the problem as other European countries and at first denied it was true cholera. But many European leaders knew how fast the cholera pandemic had traveled from the Middle East to Europe in the past, so the news of cholera in Alexandria was especially troublesome.

I had read—we all had read—about cholera. The disease, known since the sixteen hundreds, had caused deadly outbreaks across continents, mostly in places with poor living conditions and perhaps contaminated water. Cholera had occurred in the Middle East, in Russia, and even in North America and Europe. In Russia alone more than one million people had died from this disease. Cholera sometimes would cause diarrhea so severe that patients died quickly of dehydration, unable to drink enough fluids to keep up with explosive diarrhea and vomiting. It was clearly known to be contagious, spreading from one family member to another rapidly. Folklore about the disease was promulgated everywhere, as were folk remedies and preventions of all kinds. But the cause of the disease was unknown—presumed to be miasma, an unfavorable atmospheric condition.

Now in 1883, with the rapid advances in the germ theory, there was hope of better understanding the disease, finding its cause, and seeking ways to prevent its deadly consequences. That was the explanation for both the French and German governments wanting to send their scientists to Alexandria. While perhaps they were concerned with the deaths of the afflicted Egyptians, their motives were more geared toward preventing potential devastation on the European continent.

The German government had told us that this was a city of two hundred thousand, with many European features: railroads, a stock exchange, museums, and theaters.

Koch, George Gaffky, and I were recruited by the German government to sail to Alexandria, microscopes in hand, as mercenary soldiers, to battle this dangerous foe and keep it from the shores of Europe. Dr. Koch was a soldier; he had fought in the Franco-Prussian War and was not about to let down his country in this new challenge. Gaffky too had experience as a soldier in the German army, side by side with Koch; he was a patriot and was eager to study another potential germ causing disease. And there was I, Jacob Pfleger, with no country, a commitment to the war against the microbes, and few who would care if I lived or died.

As we traveled from the port to our hotel, we noticed a man lying dead in the street, with others simply walking around him. We saw families carrying meager belongings in sacks as they headed to the port, presumably looking for a safer place.

We arrived at the hotel and were given an entire floor with multiple rooms and resources to help us develop a laboratory. The plan was to have autopsy specimens sent to us from around the city. We even asked to be brought experimental animals, preferably guinea pigs. We set to work, a team with experience in defining the causes of anthrax and tuberculosis, now aiming to understand cholera. The hotel was filled with frightened tourists, but few of the guests were ill, as the illness was more concentrated in the crowded parts of the city.

As with the tuberculosis work, I did express concern to Koch about our own well-being.

"Robert, we handled samples from those who died with anthrax and tuberculosis—we washed our hands in carbolic; we tried to be careful. We alone understood that these are germs that move from one person to another, that we ourselves could be among those afflicted."

Koch nodded in agreement, but he was a true soldier, a brave man who, like me, was in a war with a tiny enemy. "Jacob, none of us wants to die. We will take all precautions. The diseased tissue will be handled with care."

"We should be wearing coverings for our hands like I have seen fancy ladies do."

"Yes, something else to work on, Jacob."

"We will be especially careful about any diarrheal samples."

I did not bring up the danger of working with cholera again. We knew what had to be done, and we started our work, each of us with a microscope, each of us at times carving up dead tissue for examination.

Rarely did we leave our rooms, but one early evening, I drifted down the stairs to the lobby of the hotel to find a café.

I had seen Adrienne in my dreams often, although never as a daytime hallucination. But this was not a dream. Entering the hotel were Adrienne and a man whom I did not recognize.

Her orange hair and green eyes could not be mistaken for anyone else's. To me she was still angelic in a pale green dress. Immediately, I knew why she was here in Alexandria, in the same hotel, for she carried with her, as did the man accompanying her, a boxed microscope in addition to her suitcase.

I would have held her and told her that I had never stopped wanting to be with her, but with another person present, our greetings were more reserved. Yet I sensed that she was grateful for this opportunity. Although Adrienne stayed calm and reserved as usual, I thought that she had almost trembled at the sight of me. She was breathless. It was different this time.

"Jacob, this is Dr. Thullier, who works with me and Dr. Pasteur. Dr. Thullier has been working in Pasteur's lab now for three years as the leader of the animal vaccination project."

Thullier was a young man; his black beard appeared like a dense mask around half his face. He did not seem to want to make eye contact and had nothing to say.

Adrienne continued, "You might have guessed why we are here. We have been sent by the French government to help identify the cause of cholera. And I suspect that you are here for the same reason."

"And Pasteur?" I asked.

"He could not make the trip and is very busy with his new rabies project."

"His health?"

"He has never truly recovered from his stroke, and we convinced him that it would not be a good idea to make this trip. But how he would have loved to speak with you again!"

During this moment in the hotel of a foreign country, surrounded by a dangerous disease and standing in front of the woman whom I had cared about like no other, I could not find the words to express that I was overwhelmed, devastated perhaps, but also hopeful that I had been given another chance in life to work with Adrienne.

Adrienne moved away from Dr. Thullier, enough to speak with me privately.

"Jacob, we need to take this strangest crossing of paths to talk. Times have changed. I will not lead the Pasteur team; that will be done by a Dr. Roux or Chamberlain. But besides that, I have so regretted our last conversation. I have missed you, tried in every way to learn what you were doing, thought of you always. Every time there was something new in the lab, I would wonder what you would say. I tried to have the same enthusiasm for our work that you always had."

I was ecstatic about her expression of care for me. I knew it was not easy for her to say even as much as she had. "We can do our work here, Adrienne, and still spend time together. This can be our time to rethink our future together."

Adrienne continued as we were rejoined by Dr. Thullier. "I want you to know that Pasteur speaks of you often. Perhaps neither of us truly understood your impact on the laboratory. Your story of childbed fever influenced him to work with the Paris Lying-in Hospital. There, women were dying of puerperal fever, which is the same as childbed fever but with a different name."

"Yes, Adrienne, that such women are still dying since Semmelweis's warning is tragic. But I have learned that new ideas are hard to sell, sometimes even to doctors or other scientists. I will call it the Semmelweis reflex—the instinct to reject new ideas for old norms."

Adrienne nodded in agreement. "Pasteur has been devastated by the criticism that has been directed against him for opposing the principle of spontaneous generation."

"And I have seen opposition to Lister's antiseptic treatments and to Koch's discovery of the anthrax bacteria."

"Pasteur wanted you to know about an important meeting that we both attended. He would have sent you a note, but he was hesitant to track you down in Germany. He has not gotten on well with Robert Koch, but that is a story for another time."

"But you say he has studied childbed fever?"

"Yes, we studied the lochia, the vaginal discharge of those women who died of the puerperal fever. We have much better microscopes now, as I know you must have as well. We have also started to isolate pure bacterial colonies on gels. The bacteria we isolated are what are now beginning to be recognized as streptococci, appearing as chains of cocci under the microscope."

The cause of childbed fever had been confirmed in the Pasteur laboratory; my suspicion was now confirmed. Couldn't that be all that was necessary to quench my passion to identify the diseases caused by microbes?

"Anyway," said Adrienne, "it was at the French Academy of Science in Paris in 1879. A physician named Hervieux was presenting at the meeting, and he stated that the epidemic at the hospital was caused by puerperal miasma. Louis Pasteur rose to face the audience, and he whispered to me that this was for Jacob and, more importantly, for Semmelweis.

"He said, 'Miasma, bad air, did not cause the epidemic. It is the nursing and medical staff who carry the microbes from an infected woman to a healthy one.' There was silence, but Pasteur's words have spread across Europe to Vienna.

"'But there is more,' Hervieux replied. 'Most respected, sir, if that is true, then I am quite sure if the germ has not been found by now, it will never be found.'

"And then Pasteur went to the blackboard, drew a very long-chained cocci, and said, 'It has been found—streptococci—and this is what it looks like.'"

Adrienne was as close to a soulmate as I would ever get, but she could never truly understand what her words on this day meant to me. I knew that the science of bacteria was changing fast, spurred by the work of Pasteur, Lister, and Koch, but knowing that Pasteur had determined the cause of my mother's death definitively, as well as the deaths of so many women around the world, changed my life's trajectory.

"Adrienne," said Dr. Thullier, "we must set up our laboratory quickly. We must represent the Pasteur laboratory and France in finding the microbe causing cholera."

"Good luck with your laboratory," Adrienne said to me, but she was no longer seemingly all business.

Adrienne and I met each evening with the background of death and disease all around us. We waited for cholera specimens, but the autopsy materials were inconsistent, and despite better German and French microscopy, no clear-cut microbes were seen in either the lung or liver tissues. While we waited for a definitive identification of the organism that caused cholera, we were given time together.

We used this gift of time to be like normal people. We walked the streets of Alexandria, hand in hand, despite the city's danger. We found new foods from Alexandria's street carts—rice, lentils, and chickpeas in chili and vinegar sauce, reheated to levels of pasteurization. As we explored the city of Alexandria, sipped coffee in outdoor cafés, or sometimes just sat in the hotel lobby, we appreciated each other and communicated in a new and different way.

"We are no different from other young people in love," I boldly suggested.

"Jacob, we have experienced more of life together than most others."

"We met and joked with Napoleon," I remembered.

"We sat side by side for weeks looking at germs on silkworms," Adrienne said with a smile. "And we found the germ."

"Actually, two different animalcules."

"Remember the faces of the cultivators when they first saw us?" Adrienne said with a laugh. Then she became serious. "We mourned the death of Pasteur's daughter together, and we learned the strength and love of family from the Pasteur family."

"I was brought up with no family and no one supporting me," I said, "and I know that it has forever affected me in a negative way. Sometimes I did not know the right thing to say or best way to behave, but I have overcome much of that deprivation. Nevertheless, I recognize the importance of family and upbringing. I would love to meet your family someday, Adrienne."

She did not respond.

"Adrienne, this is my last hunt for microbes. With Pasteur's discovery of streptococci as the cause of childbed fever, I am ready to start a new life, study in America, and become the very best doctor— but also to be with you anywhere you want to be."

"Jacob, even a new life in America is starting to sound good to me."

The next evening, we broke away from the hotel laboratories and the surrounding chaos in the streets of Alexandria and walked past the port of our arrival to the shore of the Mediterranean Sea.

The sweltering heat of the city was cooled by the sprays of the sea as waves crashed against large, irregular granite rocks. As we sat down on a rare flat rock to talk, slowly getting drenched by the sea and by a light rain, it seemed like the great expanse of the blue Mediterranean had given us the setting finally to see our lives more clearly, through a better perspective.

Adrienne, like always, was beautiful in a pale blue dress, but I could see more of the pain in her green eyes than I had seen before, and the asymmetry of her freckles along her cheeks had never been quite as pronounced before, nor had the lines around her eyes.

"Jacob, it may not be too late for us. The misery of this microbe hunt reminds us of the sacrifices we have both made."

"I want to be more like normal people, to continue our work but to find joy in life as well. I even have come to believe that is what my mother would want for me."

"Neither of us will be like normal people, but we can enjoy life like normal people do."

"Adrienne, why is it that you say I will never be normal? Is it because of my days in the orphanage?"

Adrienne smiled. "Jacob, yes, the orphanage, without the love of parents, leaves an emptiness that cannot be filled. But I believe you were born to be different. Maybe your mother's childbed fever affected your mind." She laughed as she finished that comment, and I was able to laugh too. "You have a genius for many things; that is the great part of you—and of course your ability to predict the future."

"Adrienne, I could never see you as different, only as wonderful. What makes you different in your own mind?"

"I may have just worked too hard and focused too much on my work with Louis, not thinking about a life of my own. There are other issues, Jacob, but not for now."

"Adrienne, they need us here for a bit longer, to identify the germ and grow it on plates. Then we can find a new life."

"So, Jacob, with your powers to predict the future, tell me what our sons and daughters will be like."

I thought about the question, but somehow, I could not really see that future. By this time, Adrienne was drenched from the waves, and I would always remember how in that moment in the sunset, she looked more beautiful than ever.

"Jacob, it is not too late for us. We need to leave Alexandria."

But the idea was fleeting. We had always worked at the highest level of responsibility and self-sacrifice. We had always finished the job we started, and we would see this one through as well, representing our countries of France and Germany. By the next morning, we were back at work.

As the teams separately struggled to obtain samples, ironically the outbreak was receding, giving us more time together.

Both teams began to look at diarrheal samples. And soon, almost simultaneously, with the oil immersion lenses, we found them. They were different from anything we had seen before—small rods, curved, at times in heavy concentrations, nothing like the anthrax rods, the cocci chains, or the fine beads of tuberculosis. The deadly cholera microbes looked more like little commas. The animalcules moved in a unique way, as if to quiver. Koch called them vibrios.

No one wanted to spend any more time in Alexandria. Koch and I had plated samples and appeared to have colonies on the agar we had been using. A few guinea pigs had been inoculated, but they had not come down with disease. Our work was more advanced than Thullier and Adrienne's, but both teams had felt the success of proving that cholera too was caused by a microbe, an animalcule, a germ.

Adrienne and I continued seeing each other every night. Perhaps the best idea was for me to return to France with her, to speak with Pasteur, to see the work on puerperal fever. Adrienne had suggested that we all study the next infectious disease intervention—vaccination.

"You know, Jacob, ever since you told Pasteur about the red-face disease outbreak that you saw in the orphanage and asked him about why the children would only get the disease once, when years later it would come back to get those children that it had not affected previously—"

I interrupted, "He wants to give the infection artificially to prevent it from occurring at all. Adrienne, if you want to be together in Paris, to live together, to marry, I will study anything that you choose."

However, Adrienne was not destined to leave Alexandria as planned. I was the first to develop diarrhea—it was constant and watery diarrhea—but there was plenty of water to drink, and I maintained my fluid balance. Koch remained well, having been the most careful of all of us in handling specimens.

But Dr. Thullier became quite ill with vomiting and diarrhea and was unable to keep down any fluids. We isolated him in a separate room, on a separate floor of the hotel. Koch, the German, stopped his work to help care for the Frenchman. Gaffky bravely scoured the city and found, through various connections, spearmint, chamomile, and castor oil. None of these medicines, however, slowed the loss of fluids. Thullier became weaker each day, unable to even sit up. Koch, Gaffky, Adrienne, and I did our best to care for him. He began to remind me of Paul, dizzy on standing, breathing more and more rapidly, showing bizarre behavior.

We tried to keep our hands clean, but the mess of stool and vomit was unimaginable. There was a smell of excrement and death despite our best efforts. As we cared for Thullier, we all noticed the fear on each other's faces.

And then as Thullier's condition seemed hopeless, Adrienne too became ill. Thullier's death was ghastly. But I will never be able to describe the reality of the following week. Koch was a fine doctor, but as I had seen before, doctors had no idea how to combat microbes, and his medications had not only no effect but also no rationale for use.

I never left Adrienne's bedside. I gave her water and liquids by the spoonful. She was dignified in illness and at one point, delirious or not, expressed her love for me.

"Jacob," she said, "start a new life like you intended. Leave the animalcules for someone else. You have done enough." Her eyes appeared sunken, her face paler than usual, her hair matted.

I will just say that the microbes that I had spent my life fighting, the animalcules that had killed my mother, also took the one person in my life that I truly cared about. They left me lost, defeated, and alone.

History would remember that the French commission that had been sent to Alexandria, Egypt, to combat cholera died as martyrs in the fight against infectious diseases. Koch, a German physician who had fought against the French, arranged for the cremation, for sanitation reasons, and gave me the remains of both Dr. Louis Thullier and Adrienne, which I agreed to return to France.

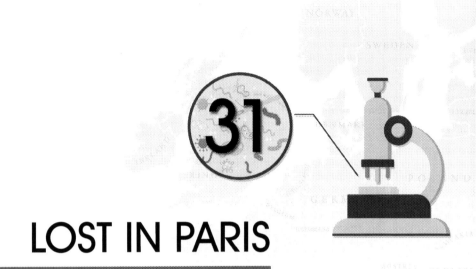

LOST IN PARIS

To my surprise, Drs. Koch and Gaffky decided to leave Alexandria, where the outbreak was cooling down, and go to India, where it was again reaching catastrophic proportions. Because we could not grow the organism consistently or find an animal model for it, they wanted to be where there were more specimens. The deaths of Adrienne and Dr. Thullier had not dissuaded them from proving that cholera was an infectious disease. Anthrax and tuberculosis were not enough for Koch. His bravery had surpassed my own naive but adventurous spirit.

I saw Dr. Koch for the last time in the port of Alexandria. We were headed in different directions. Koch looked tired, disheveled. I noted for the first-time traces of gray in his hair and beard. He appeared gaunt and had lost weight but had the same intensity in his eyes. I suspected that he hadn't slept well, that he was worried about his wife and daughter, but he was a man driven and obviously fearless.

"Jacob, you must continue this amazing journey that we have begun together. I will need your help in India."

"I cannot go on at this time. I am in mourning. And I have accomplished as much as an orphan from the Vienna Foundlings can be expected to contribute."

"Jacob, I know you are devastated by the death of this woman whom you never even mentioned to me. But you will get over her death, and you will want to continue in this new era of understanding of your animalcules."

"I will return to France, but only to pay my respects to Mr. Pasteur, to deliver the remains of Dr. Thullier, and to return the remains of Adrienne to her parents. Dr. Koch, you have been a brother to me and an inspiration. I am in awe of your love of science and medicine. Perhaps someday I will have your courage and wisdom. Please convey my goodbyes to Emmy and to Gertrude."

I set sail for France, with sadness, carrying the cremated remains of two heroes in the war against microbes.

I found Dr. Pasteur in Paris, in the Pasteur Institute. The French government was supporting his study of vaccination, and his interest had turned to rabies. He had many new colleagues and multiple laboratories. He knew in advance of my visit and of the death of his assistants.

Pasteur was hardly recognizable to me. True, I had not seen him for seventeen years. Walking had already become difficult for him back then, after his first stroke, but his second stroke had left him unsteady of gait and hunched over.

There was some irony in the fact that a world leader in the quest to understand microbes had lost two daughters to typhoid and two assistants to cholera. Pasteur sat at his desk. There were many new microscopes surrounding the room. There were animal cages, which he had not used in my time there. The room was filled with sadness, regret, and guilt.

"I should never have let them go," he whispered. "But we were too proud, too confident to say no to the French government. And Adrienne wanted to go. She had become much like you, with an intensity to serve and to break the mystery of the germs that we had discovered."

"Sir, I share the guilt. We were so preoccupied with the rebirth of our relationship that perhaps we were not as careful as we should have been."

"Jacob, the Germans had no deaths. Were you more sophisticated in your work than my group?"

"No, we were all doing the same work," I said, but I feared that our team indeed might have spent more time in washing our hands. "I have brought the ashes to give to the Thullier family and to ask you about Adrienne's family."

"Adrienne's family?"

"I know so little about them."

"That is because Adrienne had no family. She was abandoned in the Paris Hospice orphanage, where about half of all the illegitimate newborns in Paris can be found. At that time there was no adoption and abandoning a child on the street was usual. She was once able to see the form signed by her mother making the abandonment official. She had a difficult time there, and she confided in me about the level of abuse of young girls.

"But much like you, she was able to study and excel as a student, and she was recommended to me as a laboratory assistant while she studied at the university. Jacob, I did not appreciate the extent of your relationship until you left, after which she confided in me that perhaps she should have gone with you to Scotland. How you could not know about her background baffles me. But she was perhaps ashamed of her hospice orphanage experience and worried that it would have an everlasting negative effect. I cannot try to explain why she kept that from you.

"As for Thullier, his family is in Amiens, and I will be visiting them as soon as possible. He was a fine man, very quiet, a true scientist. He would never have thought of himself as martyred to this cause. He will always be a hero to the French people."

"Louis, I am so lost."

"We have both experienced great sadness and loss. But if we consider what we have done for science, what we have done for the well-being of others—you may find a happiness in thinking that you have contributed in some way to progress and the good of humanity. But whether or not our efforts are or are not favored by life, let us be able to say we have done what we could. The future will belong to those who have done the most for humanity." After a pause, Pasteur asked, "And Jacob, have you read the works of Tennyson?"

"I have not."

"Well, he said something to the effect that "Tis better to have loved and lost than to never have loved at all.'"

I actually forced a grateful smile.

"Jacob, stay as long as you like. I am in a mess with regard to trying to understand rabies—can't find the microbe at all. You could help me as in the past. A new institute is in the planning stages, and the idea of preventing microbes by vaccination will become a new commitment in France."

"Louis, I need to find a new life, certainly not here, with the memories of Adrienne. How much do you know about America, about Philadelphia?"

PHILADELPHIA

sailed from the Port of Marseille to New York City in 1884 with a ticket easily affordable from Dr. Lister's gift. Then I went by train to Philadelphia with a letter of introduction from Dr. Welch. Shortly after arrival, I took an entrance exam, which I must admit was quite elementary. I also wrote an essay on why I wanted to pursue medicine, saying that I wanted to learn science to help people.

Perhaps I was grasping to find new meaning in my life; to find a way to pursue science but to also engage with people—patients, professors; to learn to enjoy life like other people did.

Philadelphia was unlike Scotland or Germany. It was a city of increasing industry—coal, railroads, steel production—with immigrants like me from Europe trying to fit into what they called a genteel society. Philadelphia had been plagued with outbreaks of tuberculosis and malaria, perhaps caused by immigration. Rumor was that an employer would invite you to dinner, serve you a cherry pie, and see if you knew how to handle the pits.

The University of Pennsylvania's medical school was one of the best in the country but very inbred, with few of the faculty coming from outside the state. The school had made the curriculum a three-year program, like Harvard Medical School had done, and in some cases, graduation was even quicker. Medical school in the United States, as in most of Europe, was unregulated. The first two years included anatomy dissection, pharmacy, public health, and chemistry.

Already, the University of Pennsylvania medical school was going to be different, just as Dr. Welch had stated; it would be changed by Dr. William Osler, an outsider from Canada, a previous professor at McGill. I learned that Osler, just like Welch, had spent time in Germany and France learning about the newest breakthroughs in microbiology and microscopy.

We began our training in the anatomy lab, dissecting the muscles of the back, which had been determined to be the least emotionally challenging for new medical students. This was an ideal way to become acquainted with fellow students, as dissection was a team activity. Of the sixty students, two had fainting spells related to the smell of formaldehyde or just the idea of cutting open a human body. I was the first to come to their aid, and I let them know that I had had a similar experience.

We were first introduced to Dr. Osler two weeks after the anatomy class had begun. The man who I had been told on several occasions was destined for greatness, perhaps to be the greatest doctor ever, appeared much like an ordinary man with his broad forehead, black hair very neatly combed back, dark bushy mustache covering both lips, and black jacket with open collar. What was unique as he addressed the class was his manner: he was serious but amusing; had a twinkle in his eye like he would like to say something funny; and seemed just a bit nervous, as if recognizing that what he was about to say to us was important. He was the first physician that we had been exposed to since starting our program, and so the class became unusually quiet.

"It is no idle challenge that we physicians have thrown out to the world when we claim that our mission is of the highest and most noble kind, not only in combating disease but in educating the people on the laws of health and in preventing the spread of plagues and pestilence. Not that we all live up to the highest ideals—far from it, for we are only men. But we have ideals that are realizable.

"The processes of disease are so complex that it is excessively difficult to search out the laws that control them. Today we are seeing a complete revolution in our ideas; what has been accomplished is only the start of what the future has in store. The three great advances of this century have been the knowledge of controlling epidemic disease, the introduction of anesthesia, and the adoption of the antiseptic methods in surgery. The study of the causes of infectious disorders has led directly to the discovery of methods for their control; for example, the scourge of typhoid fever becomes almost unknown in the presence of an uncontaminated water supply. The outlook, too, for specific methods of treatment of these affectations is most hopeful. And it is no vain fantasy that before the twentieth century is very old, there will be effective vaccines against many contagious diseases. It cannot be denied that we have learned more rapidly how to prevent than how to cure disease. But with a definite outline of our ignorance, we no longer live in a fool's paradise and fondly imagine that in all cases we will control the issue of life and death with our pills and potions.

"Our physicians will need a clear head and a kind heart. Your work is arduous and complex, requiring the exercise of the highest faculties of the mind while constantly appealing to the emotions and finer feelings.

"It is our duty to fit men for this calling, so it will be your highest mission, students of medicine, to carry on the never-ending warfare against disease and death—to be better-equipped, abler men than your predecessors but animated with their spirit and sustained by their hopes.

"A great medical center is one to which men will flock for sound learning, whose laboratories will attract the ablest students, and whose teaching will go out to all lands.

"Best of luck to all of you, and I look forward to seeing you on the wards and in the clinics. And remember that your practice of medicine will be an art, not a trade, a calling, not a business, a calling in which your heart will be exercised equally with your head. Often the best part of your work will have nothing to do with potions and powders but will be about the exercise of the strong upon the weak, the righteous upon the wicked, and the wise upon the foolish."

My class politely applauded—all men, all younger than my thirty-six years. But for me, Osler's words gave me back what I thought I had lost. And although I would always have my aura of loneliness, I felt that maybe I belonged to a cause greater than myself that I had long been prepared to join.

My classmates had various backgrounds. Some had attended college, some just high school. A few, like me, had had no formal education and had gained admission only on the basis of having passed the entrance exam. Most were in their early twenties, but a few were in their mid-thirties. Some came from Philadelphia, and a few from New York and New Jersey. Although we were all busy studying books and lecture notes, there were other activities as well, most of which I was unprepared for. An eight-oared rowing team raced against other colleges, and I would join my classmates in rooting them on to a few victories. I joined the Hayes Agnew Surgical Society and was even invited to speak about my experiences in Glasgow, experiences that were met with skepticism. There were social fraternities, and I joined Delta Epsilon in my increasing attempt to fit in and live more fully. Most meetings revolved around heavy drinking on the Friday after an exam and debating the idea to admit women into the medical profession. I also joined the Young Men's Christian Association, trying to reevaluate my early religious experiences.

As we began our basic science training, I was quite surprised at how fast, for the most part, my European work had traveled to America. We studied the germ theory of Pasteur and the importance of pasteurization in an overall policy of public health. Of course, I always remained quite humble and never admitted to having invented the germ theory, pasteurization, the anthrax proof of cause, or surgical antisepsis.

It had become well established, with many contributions from around the world, that specific bacteria did in fact cause specific diseases. Streptococci caused skin infections, and staphylococci caused accumulation of pus. Semmelweis's work, I would soon learn, was still a controversy in the Unites States. Prominent Philadelphia obstetricians such as Drs. Hugh Hodge and Charles Meigs had been vehemently opposed to the concept of childbed fever as an infectious disease. However, a lecture titled "On the Noncontagious Character of Puerperal Fever" had been deleted from the curriculum. That lecture had reminded students of the value and dignity of the profession and sought to remove the fear that doctors could ever be ministers of evil. Now we learned of the work of the American Oliver Wendell Holmes and were provided a description of Pasteur's work that showed, in fact, that streptococci caused this disease that had killed so many American women.

As the two years of lectures came to an end, all students began to work at the University of Pennsylvania hospital, a hospital meant specifically for the teaching of medical students. When a patient was admitted to the medical service of the hospital, we were assigned to see the patient, obtain a history of illness, and later present the case to the attending physician. I was assigned to an Osler patient.

Osler met me outside of the patient's hospital room. Most of his teaching occurred at the patient's bedside. Now I had an opportunity to speak with the master physician.

"Jacob, I have already heard about your unusual background and your experience with Robert Koch, who has contributed so much to our understanding of infectious diseases."

"Dr. Osler, I have been in the operating room with Lister, in the exam room with Koch, and in the laboratory with Pasteur. I have met with Semmelweis in Vienna and have fought cholera in Egypt."

"That is quite the story. So why are you here in Philadelphia today?"

"I think it is to find myself, to belong to something, to be become the best physician. My mother and my girlfriend or fiancée died of infectious disease while the best doctors looked on and could do nothing. Some doctors are kind and compassionate but know very little that is scientifically helpful, so I want to learn to be a great physician and use scientific principles to cure disease."

"You may be asking for too much. There have been phenomenal strides in every branch of medicine. Search the scriptures of human achievement, and you cannot find any to equal the beneficence of the introduction of anesthesia, sanitation, and aseptic technique, of which you are quite aware. But Jacob, if you are looking for pills and potions to cure our newly defined infectious diseases, for that you may need to find patience.

"We are asking too much of our medical students. We need to teach them how to observe and give them plenty of facts to observe, and the lessons will come out of the facts themselves. However, experience with patients is key to learning, and that is how we will change medical education.

"Jacob, have you learned the bones of the wrist yet?"

"Yes, we have learned all 206 bones of the skeleton."

"Well, a student may know all about the bones of the wrist—in fact, he may carry a set in his pocket and know every facet and knob and nodule on them—and yet when he is called to see Mrs. Jones, who has fallen on the ice and broken her wrist, he may not know a Colles fracture from a Pott's fracture.

"So it is a safe rule to assume that we need a patient for a text. And the best teaching is provided by the patient himself. The whole art of medicine is in observation, to educate the eye to see, the ear to hear, and the finger to feel. But this takes time.

"Today we will see a patient with pneumonia. It is not hard to teach a student about pneumonia, how it prevails in winter and spring, how fatal it has always been, all about the germ, all about the change that the disease causes in the lung. He may become learned, deeply learned on the subject, but put him beside a case, and he may not know which lung is involved or how to find out; he may not know whether to give a dose of medicine every hour or no medicine at all; and he may not have the faintest notion whether the signs look ominous or favorable."

Old Blockley was the hospital where medical students would see patients and learn to become doctors. It was also part schoolhouse for orphans and part asylum for the mentally ill. It was overcrowded but was one of the few places in the city where indigent patients could get help. In 1884, it was improving, supported by both the Quakers and the city of Philadelphia with better lighting and sanitation, more nurses, and excellent doctors sincerely wanting to make it one of the great teaching hospitals in the country. Nurses in their new white uniforms helped bring discipline and order to the system. Many of the patients were immigrants, and many were of black skin.

The wards were large rooms with about forty patients per ward, beds lined up in rows.

I somehow found the bed number for Mr. Cole. He was a black man, older, and was sitting in bed coughing. He looked uncomfortable.

"He really needs your help, Doctor," said a younger man in a nearby bed. "He has been coughing most of the night."

I already had a good knowledge of history-taking from observing Dr. Koch, so when Dr. Osler arrived, I was ready to tell him about the patient.

"Mr. Cole is a fifty-year-old male who has complained of having a cough and fever for three days. Over the past day, he has experienced increasing shortness of breath. He smokes cigarettes but has never had an episode like this before. He lives with his wife, and she has had no similar illness."

Osler moved a chair very close to the patient's bedside, held the patient's hand, and asked him where he was from. He asked what work the patient did and how he spent his time, and when the patient noted that he liked to read, Osler explored his reading list.

"You have been coughing for several days?"

"Yes, a few days."

"And what does the material that you cough up look like?"

"Yellow, mostly."

"Mostly, but is there any blood in your sputum—that is, the material that you are coughing up?"

"No, no bright-red blood."

"But is there some rust-like sputum?"

"Yes, rust-like."

"And you feel feverish?"

"Yes, feverish."

"Have you ever had a chill such that you were so cold it made you shake?"

"Yes, I had a chill."

"A single shaking chill or many chills?"

"Just one chill."

"And what about your bedclothes?"

"Yes, I soaked them with sweat."

"And any pain when you take a deep breath?"

"Yes, I do have pain; it's hard to take a deep breath."

"Pain on one side or both?"

"Just the right side and right lower back."

"Mr. Cole, I am going to examine you with my medical student. Is that OK with you?"

"Yes, of course."

Osler proceed to do the physical exam as I watched intently. He spoke to me as he proceeded. When he came to the lung exam, he asked the patient to breathe normally and placed both his hands around the lower part of the patient's back, where the bases of the lungs would be. Osler's hand moved with the inspiration of the patient's breath, but there was less movement on the right side. Osler then percussed both bases of the lung, hammering with his fingers above the lung much as one would do to find a hollow place on a wall, proceeding from right lung to left lung, each percussion higher and higher on the back.

The left side sounded hollow like a drum where air was filling the lung, but the right side sounded flat. Osler then used his stethoscope, asking the patient to breathe deeply. He put the stethoscope to my ears, and I heard sounds that were not normal at the right base of the lung, sounds like bubbles or little dots in time. He asked the patient to say "ee," but over the right lung, the "ee" sounded like "aye."

"Jacob, the symptoms of cough and fever suggest a respiratory infection of some kind. Pain on inspiration on the right side means the right lower lobe of the lung is probably involved. A single shaking chill and rusty sputum are characteristic of one particular organism. Do you know what that would be?"

I did not know.

"We will take a sample of sputum and go the laboratory." In the lab, Dr. Osler did a series of stains. "A staining method was just developed by Hans Christian Gram," said Osler. "This is called a Gram stain. It will stain some bacteria red and others blue."

"I knew that was coming," I whispered involuntarily.

"Jacob, I need not look under the microscope to predict that this pneumonia is caused by what we call the Captain of the Men of Death; rarely do other organisms cause a single shaking chill or rusty sputum. It is the most common cause of pneumonia in the elderly, and it carries a poor prognosis."

He asked me to peer under the microscope, using the oil immersion lens that I was familiar with, but with a better staining method than Koch's.

"And what do you see?"

"Staining blue, cocci, round, in pairs."

"Note if they are more in pairs than chains."

"Yes, not like the streptococci of wounds but similar."

"Jacob, this is the Diplococci pneumoniae. We have seen and evaluated an elderly patient with Diplococci pneumoniae pneumonia."

"And how will we treat him?"

"An opioid to reduce pain will help him breathe more deeply. Fluids to prevent dehydration. Oxygen if it is needed."

"But Dr. Osler, to kill the bacteria?"

"Jacob, what would you suggest?"

"A pill, a potion that would get into the patient's bloodstream and be directed to the lung, where it would kill the invading microbes."

"Jacob, the pill you describe does not exist."

"But it could exist?"

"Yes, perhaps it could someday exist."

"Dr. Osler, do you have patients who have survived this Diplococci pneumonia?"

"Yes, of course."

"Could blood have some elements generated for the infection that could be useful to a patient who is presently infected?"

Osler smiled, saying, "Jacob, you may just become both a great doctor and a great scientist!"

I continued to see patients with the physicians of the University of Pennsylvania. With Dr. Joseph Leidy, who was our anatomy teacher, I saw a patient with diffuse muscle pain. Others were admitted to the hospital with the same problem and a common history of eating uncooked pork. Dr. Leidy performed a muscle biopsy and was an expert microscopist, as skilled as I was.

"We needed only a two hundred times magnification to see within muscle tissue a thick- walled cyst and within the cyst a curled-up worm, a larva that had spread throughout the muscles of the body," reported Dr. Leidy.

I, of course, asked Dr. Leidy how we could treat such an infection by killing the worms without injuring the patient. As with other physicians of the day, Dr. Leidy had the usual response: that we did not know of such a treatment. However, over time, Dr. Leidy said we would let the world know that there were worms in uncooked pork and that adequate cooking of the meat would prevent such an infection.

Over the course of a very busy year, I saw a variety of patients at Old Blockley with internists, surgeons, obstetricians, and psychiatrists. We students learned to extract all information from the patient's history; as Osler had said, the patient was telling us the diagnosis. We learned to hear heart sounds and lung sounds with the stethoscope, to feel an enlarged liver or spleen, and to check for lymph nodes in the neck, groin, and axilla and determine their size, shape, mobility, and texture. We learned to assess the functioning of the nerves of the body and the patient's mental status, balance, and ability to see and hear and recognize touch. And whenever a patient died, we would attend the autopsy to determine the cause of death.

While I learned something from every Old Blockley doctor, none was more valuable than Osler. I particularly remember the case of Mr. White, age thirty-six, whom I saw in my third and final year of medical school. I interviewed Mr. White at his bedside, with Dr. Osler observing me.

"And why have you come to the hospital, Mr. White?"

"For months I have had some fever and sweats. I have lost my appetite and lost weight. I have some pain on my left side. And I have some problem with my skin."

"And were you well before this illness?"

"I had arthritis, rheumatism, as a child. They say it may have affected my heart."

I examined the patient. His temperature was 100.5. He was pale and looked thin. The impulse of the heart felt in the anterior chest was displaced laterally, suggesting an enlarged heart. On listening to the heart, I detected an abnormal sound, a heart murmur. On listening to the lungs, I heard the sound of rales, suggesting fluid. I could feel the enlarged spleen with the tip of my fingers as I curled them under the rib cage and asked the patient to take a deep breath. There were crops of tiny purple spots on the patient's arms and legs— petechiae. And there were tender nodules on the tips of his fingers. On neurological exam, he was found to have some mild weakness on his left side.

"Dr. Osler, this patient is likely to have endocarditis, infection of the heart valves."

"And Jacob, how have you made that diagnosis?"

"With a prior history of rheumatism, the patient likely had rheumatic fever, which is known to damage heart valves. Sometime in the last few months, he had an episode of bacterial infection, and the bacteria settled on his damaged heart valve. The bacteria on the heart valve caused abnormalities in the valve, which then broke off in pieces. Those emboli went to the brain to cause a stroke and even to the tips of the fingers. The enlarged spleen confirms long-standing infection."

"And how will you confirm that diagnosis?"

"We are now routinely able to obtain blood cultures and grow specific bacteria."

"And Jacob, what bacteria would you suspect in this case?"

"I have read from your papers, Dr. Osler, that a variety of bacteria can cause endocarditis but that streptococci are the most likely."

The patient's blood cultures did grow streptococci. A few months later, the patient died, and at autopsy we saw the streptococci deeply embedded in his heart valve. Bacteria were seen in the nodules of the fingers and in the spleen as well.

After the autopsy, I had questions for Osler. "The lesions on the fingers—I have not read of them in endocarditis."

"They are not common, Jacob, but I have seen that occur several times. We should better describe it in the literature."

"I agree," I said with some enthusiasm. "Perhaps we should call them Osler's nodes."

Osler only smiled after the thought of naming some skin lesions after him. "Jacob, I want you to realize this disease has a 100 percent mortality rate. Bacteria continue to grow in the heart valve until the heart fails or fatal emboli go to the brain."

"Dr. Osler, perhaps we could remove the bacteria on the heart valve by surgery?"

"Yes, maybe someday that can be done."

"Or give a drug powerful enough to kill the bacteria in the heart valve?"

"Jacob, that drug would have to be in a very high concentration to get into the heart valve from the bloodstream. But I do think we agree that from here anything is possible."

Then I was ready to ask the question that I had long been hoping to ask. "Dr. Osler, I am soon to graduate. I would like to work with you and with your colleagues—to see patients together and find new treatments for them. Would that be possible?"

Osler smiled and nodded slightly but said, "Jacob, you will need to come to my meeting with the whole of the University of Pennsylvania School of Medicine next week."

JOHNS
HOPKINS

The entire school of medicine of the University of Pennsylvania had been called together to hear from Dr. William Osler. While many rumors had circulated, no one knew for sure what he was going to say.

As usual, he started out with what appeared to be general advice to his students and colleagues. "In the physician and surgeon, no quality takes rank with imperturbability, and I propose to direct you to this essential virtue. Imperturbability means coolness and presence of mind under all circumstances, calmness amid the storm, clearness of judgment in moments of peril ... It is the quality that is most appreciated by the laity, and the physician who has the misfortune to be without it, who betrays indecision and worry and who shows that he is flustered in ordinary emergencies, loses rapidly the confidence of his patients ... Cultivate then, gentlemen, such a judicious measure of aequanimitas as will enable you to meet the exigencies of practice with firmness and courage."

Osler went on to give examples of this quality of aequanimitas, as I and others wondered, why now? Why had this become a particular issue? But then the importance of the meeting became clear.

"While preaching to you on the doctrine of equanimity, I am myself a castaway. One might have thought that in the premier school in America, with associations so dear to a lover of this profession, that the Hercules Pillars of a man's ambition have been reached. But it has not been so ordained."

I knew then that Osler was leaving for the new Johns Hopkins medical school.

"Today I sever my connection with this university. I have been placed in such a position that no words could express the feelings of my heart. A stranger, an alien among you, I have been made to feel at home; more you could not have done. Nothing can quench the pride I shall always feel at having been associated with a faculty so notable and distinguished ... Gentlemen, farewell and take into the struggle the watchword 'aequanimitas.'"

It was 1887, and the much-anticipated Johns Hopkins medical school was opening. William Welch—who had directed me to Philadelphia with a letter of introduction and who had seen my collaboration with Koch—was the school's first dean and had begun to collect the most talented physicians and scientists that perhaps the world had ever known.

After the speech, Osler gathered several of us together. He needed graduating medical students to become residents, house officers, and individuals who would work closely with patients, caring for them night and day in the newly designed hospital while being supervised by the best attending physicians that could be found from around the country. It would be hard work and not likely possible for married physicians, but it would provide the education necessary for excellence in this new, rapidly advancing profession. Perhaps it would define the education of a physician in the Unites States for decades.

Osler chose Fred Packard as chief resident, but Dr. Packard's father would not let him leave Philadelphia. Dr. Henri Lafleur, who had followed Osler from Canada, would also make the trip to Baltimore. Isabel Hampton, the head nurse at the Philadelphia hospital, would leave with him as well.

Osler met with me as he left the lecture hall. "Jacob, your modesty about your contributions to medical science are appreciated. In fact, Dr. Welch specifically asked me to be sure that you would join us. Your love of science and passion to be a physician of competence is exactly what we need at the Johns Hopkins Medical School and Hospital."

Needless to say, I was ready to pack my bags and follow and work for the finest physician in America.

Johns Hopkins Hospital sat on a hill in Baltimore overlooking the Chesapeake Bay. It was a redbrick building with Victorian architecture that I had been accustomed to, particularly in Glasgow, with towers and domes and ornate windows. The wards were divided among sixteen different buildings of one or two floors. The importance of sanitation, of good ventilation, and of preventing contagious disease was a relatively new concept that would require constant adjustment.

Becoming a physician at the new medical school and working with the best clinicians, including Osler himself, refocused my passion for science. Now, in 1887, at the age of thirty-nine, I realized that my work to define the germ theory, the public health implications of pasteurization, the end of the spontaneous generation myth, the importance of antisepsis and infection control, and the Koch work to prove that bacteria caused specific diseases had truly changed the world forever.

Now the future was to recognize specific clinical findings and information that came from history-taking and physical exam to match disease presentation with specific pathogens causing disease.

At Hopkins, we began to consolidate breakthroughs from around the world that contributed to this effort. Of course, my mentor, Robert Koch, had already shown that bacteria caused anthrax and tuberculosis and that the outbreak of cholera had been caused by a vibrio. But now Theodor Escherich from Munich had defined an organism that caused diarrhea in children. Anton Wiechselbaum from Vienna had identified a Diplococcus intracellularis, stained red by the Gram stain, that was the cause of meningitis, often identifying itself clinically with the rash that it produced. Drs. Daniel Salmon and Theobald Smith had implicated a Gram-negative rod, a Salmonella bacterium, as the cause of some food poisoning and also perhaps the disease typhoid fever, which had caused the death of Pasteur's daughters. Alexander Ogston, a Scottish surgeon, confirmed my work with Lister showing that an organism now named staphylococci caused wound infections that produced pus and required drainage. And we must never forget, there was the organism causing the death of postpartum women, the cause of childbed fever, not a poison or an atmospheric condition, but a streptococcus. The animalcules were being defined, and the battle against them was moving forward.

This work was often difficult and frustrating. Pasteur had not been able to identify the organism causing rabies, a fatal brain infection following dog or wolf bites. No one had found the organism causing smallpox, not even by examining the skin blisters that it produced. I had come to believe that even with our better microscopes, there might still be microbes, animalcules, too small to see.

But our work was just beginning. Shortly after starting my work as a house officer at the new hospital, I saw a patient who was complaining of long-standing diarrhea and also right-sided stomach pain. His skin had turned yellow in color. He was a young medical student who had come from Panama.

"Dr. Jacob, diarrhea is common where I come from," said the Panamanian physician. "Sometimes many people will get sick at the same time, from drinking the same water."

"Water that is contaminated with microbes?" I asked.

"Perhaps so."

"And what have you seen to be the consequences of this illness?" I asked.

"Most get better if they have a good source of water to drink so that they do not become dehydrated."

"Yes, I understand," I replied. "It is much like the disease of cholera. But your stomach pain?"

"Yes, that has been a problem for me, right-sided stomach pain."

I examined the young student. His sclera, the white of his eyes, had taken on a muddy brown color. His skin looked slightly yellow. He had a pain in his abdomen, in the right upper quadrant. I could feel the edge of the liver. But also, drumming my finger over the right side of the chest, I noted that the normal hollow sound was gone, and the normal sounds of the lung could not be heard. That meant that there was fluid in the space between the lung and chest wall, the pleural space.

I took a stool sample to the laboratory to examine for bacteria, recognizing that we now knew there would always be many different kinds of bacteria in a stool sample.

But to my surprise, I found a phenomenon that I had never seen before. I called for both Osler and William Welch, who was now also available as the head of the laboratory.

In the stool sample there were living organisms, not small but quite large and easily identified. They looked like white blood cells but larger, and they were changing shape, moving with pseudopods.

Dr. Osler was familiar with the organism, although he had not seen it himself previously. "Yes, this was first described in St. Petersburg, Russia, in 1875, by Dr. Fedor Aleksandrovich Lesh—paradoxical, as it is usually a disease found in warm climates. He described them as amoebas and said they cannot be confused with anything else, not even for a moment, because of the way they move."

"But Dr. Osler, the patient also has involvement of the liver and lung. Perhaps by the same amoeba?"

We agreed to aspirate the pleural space, to drain the excess fluid and examine it for amoebas. The fluid was filled with the same type of amoeba, the same parasite.

Sadly, as again there was no treatment for this extensive parasitic disease, our young student developed worsening liver disease over several months and died at the Johns Hopkins Hospital surrounded by the best physicians. At autopsy, extensive involvement of the liver was found, and there was a large abscess filled with the parasite. Dr. Osler would be the first to describe amoebic dysentery with the complication of liver abscess.

"Jacob, you have heard me say that he who studies medicine without books sails an uncharted sea, but he who studies medicine without patients does not go to sea at all," said Dr. Osler. "Today we are beginning to characterize the signs and symptoms of disease faster than ever before. And you can help. I am writing everything I know about the practice of medicine, and I want your help."

"To write about what we know about disease?"

"What we know to be true, so that all physicians everywhere have the same facts to go by."

"And how will we know what is true and what is not?"

"Medicine is a science of uncertainty and an art of probability. We will, here at Hopkins, observe, record, communicate. We will use our five senses, learn to feel, learn to hear, learn to smell, and know that by experience we can become the experts."

"What diseases would you have me write about?"

"The book will be called *The Principles and Practice of Medicine*. Jacob, you can help me with tuberculosis, typhoid fever, measles, cholera, erysipelas, puerperal fever, and of course, anthrax."

"I will see patients during the day and write about disease, with you perhaps, on weekends and during vacations?"

"Yes, and Jacob, Dr. Welch also needs you in his laboratory to help correlate our diseases with laboratory findings. He has an outstanding group of young doctors who are working with him."

Reintroducing myself to William Welch was an immense pleasure. He was the medical school dean—a position that gave him the responsibility for both the education and the well-being of his students—and a brilliant and congenial man, like most medical school deans. Often, Welch would dine with us and would talk of art, music, and literature. He would encourage us to attend carnivals, to seek out old bookstores. Those of us who worked with him began to know and understand each other, working hard to be the best physicians, scientists, and human beings.

But Welch was a research scientist as well, having a deep understanding of the work of both Koch and Pasteur. He had opened his laboratory to sixteen young physicians. And I took the opportunity to continue my passion for scientific discovery, while caring for patients at the same time. Among the sixteen were Simon Flexner, Walter Reed, James Carroll, and Jesse Lazear. Flexner was absorbed with the issues of what we should learn and how. But I found a great camaraderie with Carroll and Lazear. Like me, they wanted answers to the cause of diseases, particularly those that were contagious and threatening world health. They had joined the army, where they could fight microbes around the world, but had been assigned to the Hopkins program. I sensed that their dedication was very much like mine had been.

A thirty-six-year-old patient whom I saw on the wards became a source of study in the laboratory. He had been admitted after a serious farming accident with a leg wound not unlike some I had seen with Dr. Lister. This wound had been seriously contaminated by soil, as a tractor had run over the farmer's leg, and there had been a delay in seeking care. After cleaning the wound, I examined it and found it to be very tender to the touch. It had a foul-smelling discharge, as I had seen many times before in Scotland. However, this patient was quite ill, with a very high fever and increased heart rate. What was unusual was the feeling of air under the skin, or crepitus as it was called. Using my ears, as Osler always suggested we do, I could hear a crackling sound on touching the wound. Also unusual was the condition's rapid spread along the leg as we were observing it.

William Halsted, the new leader of surgery at Johns Hopkins, was called to see the patient. Halsted prepared the patient for amputation and invited me to attend the surgery. His surgical technique was most meticulous. He described the anatomy of the leg as he proceeded with the procedure, demonstrating the same teaching skill as Welch and Osler. He was assisted by his nurse, Caroline Hampton, who was wearing rubber surgical gloves that had been made especially for her by the Goodyear rubber company.

After surgery, I made a special point of delivering the amputated portion of the leg to the Welch laboratory, as I suspected an unusual disease process. I also inquired about the gloves worn by the nurse at the time of surgery. I complimented Dr. Halsted on the use of rubber gloves in surgery and told him that for infection control purposes, I had recommended the same to Lister more than twenty years earlier.

"Jacob," said Halsted, "we designed the gloves especially for Nurse Hampton because she is allergic to mercuric chloride and carbolic acid. Washing with these solutions caused a rash on her hands. Others in the surgical suite have adopted the gloves as well."

"My recommendation, Dr. Halsted, based on years of working with the great Lister, would be that all surgical nurses everywhere should be wearing the same type of gloves to prevent the spread of infection in the operating room."

"Jacob," said Halsted with a smile, "we will surely consider that recommendation."

The following day, I studied the leg specimen with Dr. Welch. Drs. Carroll and Lazear attended as well.

The Johns Hopkins pathology laboratory was larger and more modern than any I had ever seen. Welch, Carroll, Lazear, and I gathered around a metal table with excellent overhead lighting. The portable cabinets with wheels that could move from one table to another held a wide range of surgical knives, glass slides, and solutions for the latest type of bacterial staining, Gram staining. Since my time working with Koch, using immersion oil had become routine, as had taking photomicrographs of bacteria. I made the first incision into the amputated leg. The large gastrocnemius muscle was almost liquid, entirely necrosed. A foul-smelling gas was released into the air. Even more striking were the gas bubbles clogging the arteries of the leg. Welch himself had not seen this type of rapid muscle destruction and gas production.

I took the lead in staining and studying samples of the muscle and the fluid surrounding the muscles of the leg. Bacteria were everywhere in the samples—very large rods similar to those seen in anthrax. We were later to find them in a culture much like the clostridium species that Pasteur had just described related to food poisoning, but with different biochemical characteristics, meaning a new bacteria and a new disease entity. We were excited to get back to Osler to describe a new clinical entity—gas gangrene caused by a clostridium species.

I suggested we call this microbe *Clostridium welchii*, in honor of our mentor. I believed the name would long be remembered.

After our work that morning was done, James Carroll and Jesse Lazear wanted to learn more about me, and I, more about them. With his British accent, James was obviously from England. He had joined the US Army before becoming a physician but had been assigned to his superior, Walter Reed, to work in the Welch pathology lab. Carroll was also in the military but working as a physician and scientist with Dr. Welch. Carroll, like Osler, was interested in the increasing number of cases of malaria in Baltimore.

The three of us had cared for patients together many nights in the quiet of the hospital wards. While patients were put to bed, and the nurses congregated together in their stations, we would compare notes about patients, always wondering what we might have missed and what more we could do for the failing patients. In the morning, before the senior attending physicians arrived, we would have breakfast together before sneaking off to our quarters in the hospital for a quick nap.

But today James and Jesse wanted to know who I really was.

"Jacob, the rumors about you are crazy."

"You mother died of childbed fever, and you were brought up in an orphanage?"

"That is true."

"And you knew Semmelweis?"

"I did meet him, but I was only twelve years old at the time."

"And you went from Vienna to Lille to work with Pasteur when you were only twelve?"

"Well, I went to Lille to find my father who worked in the vineyards, and then I just happened to meet Pasteur."

"And you traveled to France from Vienna by steamship?"

"Mostly, I walked along the Danube."

"And you met Pasteur and worked for him?"

"Yes, I helped him in his laboratory."

"As an untrained lab assistant?"

"Yes, but I helped him prove that microbes were causing the wine of Lille to spoil, and then I suggested to him that the bacteria might be killed by heating the wine."

"You made that suggestion?"

"Yes, and I called my idea pasteurization. I even swallowed some sour milk with bacteria in it to prove it caused illness."

"And you became ill?"

"Only mildly so. Gentlemen, my story will be difficult for you to believe, and it is not important that you do so. I also met Napoleon and promised him I would find out why the silkworms were dying, and I did that by finding the microbes responsible—working with my girlfriend."

"Ah, so you do have a girlfriend?"

"Yes, I did, but she died in Alexandria, Egypt, when we were studying the cause of cholera. She was working with Pasteur's group, and I was working with Koch. She and her colleague died as martyrs in the fight against disease and microbes. I used to call them animalcules after Leeuwenhoek, who first described them."

"But you came here from Koch's laboratory, I was told."

"I worked with him, lived in his farmhouse, and helped discover the causes of anthrax and tuberculosis. My story is simple. Once I knew my mother had died of a preventable disease caused by bacteria, I was ready to fight the battle against microbes wherever that took me."

Lazear replied, "We are privileged to be in an unprecedented age of discovery."

"A privilege and a challenge for all of us," said James Carroll.

"We have at our disposal," said Lazear, "the knowledge and tools to change the world, to better understand the diseases that kill people at an early age. And those disease are mostly those caused by bacteria."

"Well," I added, "we can celebrate that we learned about one more today—the *Clostridium welchii*."

"Jacob, it is an honor to work with you," said Dr. Lazear, and Dr. Carroll nodded in agreement.

"Let's make a pact together that our lives in this special time of enlightenment will be dedicated to changing the course of mankind by preventing microbial diseases," I said.

And we raised our coffee mugs in celebration of our commitment.

"Jacob," Lazear asked, "were you prepared to die from your sour milk to prove a point about microbes?"

CELEBRATING
PASTEUR

From house officer, I became a practicing physician at the Johns Hopkins Hospital, caring for the underserved, working under difficult conditions, and teaching medical students. Like others in academic medicine, I combined patient care, scholarship, and medical student teaching. Teaching students the profession of medicine and modeling my work after the great teacher William Osler was a joy. There was no greater feeling of achievement than showing a medical student how to actually feel a spleen tip or see the jugular vein abnormally distended, how to see the impulse of the heart through the chest wall, or how to find a perforation in an eardrum. But even more thrilling was to hear from the patient some subtle clue to the diagnosis. As Osler had said, the patient would tell us the diagnosis if we listened.

I also continued to seek out reliable treatments for microbial diseases. Yes, it was true that recognizing that germs caused disease would in itself result in many types of prevention, including the new field of vaccination led by the Pasteur Institute, but we were making little progress on my dream of treating each disease with an effective drug. At Hopkins we were excited to hear the report from the Koch laboratory that a cure for tuberculosis had been discovered. It was called tuberculin and was made up of the material of the tubercle bacillus itself. In true Oslerian spirit, we treated our tuberculosis patients with tuberculin and carefully recorded the outcomes, including days of fever, cough, weight gain, and mortality. We compared the treated group to the untreated group. Sadly, there was no effect. The effective treatment of tuberculosis was likely still decades away.

After many years practicing at Hopkins, I began to feel the joy of belonging, as it was hard to feel alone when thrown into the sea of human suffering, disability, and tragedy, but also rehabilitation, patient courage, miracles, resilience, and the nobility of the patient spirit. But I did also miss those great days of discovery. That was why I was very pleased to be invited to Louis Pasteur's seventieth birthday party in 1892, to be celebrated at the Sorbonne. With the relative ease of travel compared to the past, and because I had made a decent living, with my money mostly saved, I looked forward to returning to Europe, almost as a vacation, to see my old mentors and celebrate their success.

I arrived in Paris the night before the Pasteur celebration. Being in Paris brought back my years in France, including my work with Adrienne in studying the silkworms and the days I spent with Pasteur in his home, heating the microbes in wine. But my sadness was turning into an appreciation for those times Adrienne and I did have, and although I had been advised by so many to stop and smell the flowers, I realized that my contentment in life would be my work. I was neither Osler nor Welch when it came to cultivating appreciation for the arts and other finer points of life.

The theater in which the Pasteur party was held was meant to hold 2,500 people, but it was overcrowded with scientists and friends from all over the world. The guests included ambassadors from many countries; statesmen from around the world; the president of France, Sadi Carnot; and the entire staff of the Pasteur Institute. Professors from many countries attended in academic dress and colorful gowns and hoods. The gargantuan theater was spectacular, with its Greek mythology murals and ancient sculptures.

Pasteur entered the theater at 10:30 a.m., appearing old and debilitated to a rapturous standing ovation. He was assisted onto the podium by the French president. Pasteur, never fully recovered from his stroke, walked slowly, debilitated by sorrow, frustration, and conflict. Those discoveries that we had quietly made in his modest laboratories were now appreciated not only by scientists but also by all of those who had been affected: silkworm curators, wine growers, farmers, and all who had feared anthrax and tuberculosis.

Joseph Lister, who had come from London, where he now led the elite British surgical program, also received a thunderous ovation as he rose to speak about Pasteur. Lister graciously gave credit to Pasteur for the rapid improvements in surgical technique around the world. Pasteur reclaimed the podium to give Lister a kiss on each cheek.

I felt some sadness that Dr. Robert Koch was not in attendance, but I knew that the Franco-Prussian War and some debate about anthrax and its vaccine had resulted in disputes and a rift between him and Pasteur that could not be healed. Despite their feud, I knew that they would be remembered together as great partners in defining bacteria and the diseases they caused.

However, I would have liked to have moved to the podium, to introduce myself as the son of a woman physician who had died of childbed fever and who with Ignaz Semmelweis had let the world know of a tragic gap in scientific knowledge—Leeuwenhoek's animalcules existed and were causing disease and death not only in women giving birth but also in patients all over the world. Ignaz, had he not died of depression and melancholy, could have been at this party at age seventy-four.

Among the huge crowds, I stood in line to have a word with both Lister and Pasteur, and I did have my moment. Although I received a gracious hug and recognition from both of them, I understood that to both, I was just a former laboratory assistant, and there were ambassadors and presidents in the room. In fact, they were right: I had been a laboratory assistant with no real training—perhaps one with the right ideas, but ideas were easy, and scientific truth was a more difficult journey.

More importantly, I realized that with all the great respect I had for both of them, there were still so many besides me who had been part of the science of discovery, over many years, many countries, and many cultures, whose work would never be truly recognized.

Also in attendance were students interested in science from all over Europe—students of the Sorbonne, students from French high schools and colleges, and some from London and Glasgow as well. One young group, teenagers from the Royal Polytechnic Institution in London, were attending as part of their science class.

"Sir," began one of the young men, a wide-eyed, brown-haired, curious fellow wearing a blue Polytechnic jacket, "so you must know Dr. Lister? At least well enough to shake his hand?"

"Yes, enough to shake his hand today, but I also worked with him for many years."

"In Scotland?"

"Yes, in Glasgow."

"That is where I was born and raised," said the young boy. "Just moved to London to begin the study of science."

"Never too early to study science," I said as I shook the young man's hand and smiled. "I began when I was a bit younger than you are now. Why the study of science for you?"

"Well, growing up in Scotland, we learned of Lister and his great discoveries to fight microbes. So all Scottish children were inspired by him."

"I have studied microbes from the time I was your age—with Pasteur and Lister and with Koch as well."

"And who inspired you?" the young man asked.

I was in no hurry and so told him a bit of my story: my mother's death, the spoiled wine, and the silkworms, plus a mention of anthrax. I must say he was openmouthedly curious.

"So we are winning the war against microbes?" he asked.

"No, nothing of the sort. We know what they do but not really how to kill them effectively. Perhaps that will be the work of your generation."

"I would like to be a part of that."

"Well, what is your name? Perhaps we can stay in touch as you study science at the Royal Polytechnical. My name is Jacob."

"Yes, I will do that, sir. My name is Alexander. Alexander Fleming."

"Good to meet you, Alexander. Study, learn, and ask questions, Alexander. Always ask the right questions, the questions others have not thought to ask. Work hard, and someday you too might make a great discovery, perhaps after years of planning or perhaps just by chance."

I then excused myself to leave the theater. Sensing that this might well be my last visit across the ocean, I had several more stops to make. I wanted to visit the Pasteur Institute to touch the memorial plaques for Adrienne and Thullier. I also wanted to go to Lille, to bid farewell to my aging father and my half brother and to introduce myself to his wife and children.

When I arrived in Lille, I was in awe of the expanding healthy vineyards, and during my visit I took time to hike through the hills with the whole group and even tried again the challenge of fishing, to glimpse the life that had not been my chosen path.

From Lille, the trip to Vienna was different than my journey had been forty years ago.

RETURN TO VIENNA

Vienna was my birthplace, no matter how unfortunate my early life might have been. I was a self-trained scientist and well-trained physician now, at age forty-four, and had accomplished some of what I had set out to do. Vienna was calling me back to see it one more time: the hospital, my childhood friend, and the staff of the Vienna General Hospital.

I met Neil at the Vienna train station. The last time I'd seen him was the night before I left for Lille, when I was aged twelve; Neil had been older, although his date of birth and the names of his parents had never been known. I easily picked him out in the crowded train station even though more than forty years had passed. His brown hair was now mostly gray, though still it covered much of his forehead. He was tall still, but his gawky posture was gone, and like most middle-aged men, he looked heavier around the middle. He had on a white coat and looked as professional as my Johns Hopkins colleagues. Neil also had no trouble spotting me.

As we walked to a café close to the train station, I knew that there was an enduring bond between us, forged by twelve years of common orphanage experience.

Neil began by describing his training in both dermatology and pediatrics. He had become the physician for the Vienna Foundlings. As he spoke, I recognized the same slowness of speech, the same careful choosing of words, from our childhood.

"It is a different life here," he said. "Vienna has become a city of great culture, innovations, and breakthroughs in the fields of medicine, literature, art, and music. The Vienna Medical School may be the best in Europe." By now two million residents had settled in the city from the multinational Habsburg empire.

I had so many questions. "What do you know of Hebra and Skoda? I would like to thank them for coming to see me at the orphanage. It was a wish of my mother's, but one they chose to honor."

"Both dead, long ago."

"My mother's friend Hannah?"

"Died just recently, but always asked about you. Jacob, you have been gone for an exceptionally long time. Why return now?"

"To see you, Neil."

"That is good to know. And I have wanted to see you as well, to let you know that I too made it out of the orphanage. We both might be seen as having some resilience. I care for the children there now. There are many fewer drop-offs there, more adoptions, and better overall care."

"Is the red-face disease still a problem?" I asked.

"Well, we both know that that is called measles now. It is so contagious and on occasion deadly in a few children who develop pneumonia. But you must know, Jacob, none of your animalcules can be found with that disease."

"Too small to be seen. Same with rabies, even smallpox. No germs. But there is a Russian botanist working right now on tobacco plants that are diseased. He can use a filter, letting only the smallest particles through it, and still show the material remains contagious. They don't have a name yet, but they won't be called bacteria."

Returning focus back to the orphanage, I asked, "And how does a pediatrician handle such a disease?"

"We isolate the first case, and all who touch the patient wash their hands. We still have outbreaks, but they are less severe."

"What about the winter death that is now called typhus? The creatures that we saw on the children were lice, lice that spread disease."

"We don't see that problem in the orphanage anymore," said Neil. "With just better care—clean clothes, better nutrition—it seems to be gone. Jacob, would you like to see the orphanage?"

I did not answer.

"Jacob, what do you need me to do for you? I am so glad to see you, but you did not come here from Lille just to see me after thirty years."

"I am a physician at one of the best hospitals in the United States. I would like to address the doctors at the Vienna hospital. Can you arrange that, Neil?"

"Yes, of course. We have weekly conferences. Many have heard that you were responsible for the great breakthroughs with Pasteur, Lister, and Koch. However, most do not really believe that a Viennese orphan was part of those great discoveries."

"I don't blame them. In fact, they also were made by many others whose names will never be known—faculty associates and laboratory workers."

"You do realize, Jacob, that your name does not appear on publications or in the programs of conferences?"

"Yes, Neil, that has never been of great importance to me. There are too many arguments already on who is to take credit. It is part of the reason that Koch and Pasteur will not speak to each other."

"I will set up a time for your address. It will be well attended."

"And can you get it done soon, Neil? I am anxious to return to the United States."

The large, traditional conference room was much like the ones in Glasgow or Paris, and in fact it was the same conference room to which I had come at age twelve to meet Semmelweis and hear Lister speak. Audience members filled the room the same way they had back in 1860: older, well-dressed doctors in the front row and younger, more boisterous physicians and students in the back rows overlooking the central area and podium. I had not given a speech before, not even in Philadelphia or Baltimore, but somehow, I had prepared what I wanted to say for decades.

Neil introduced me as a visiting professor, a medical doctor graduated from the University of Pennsylvania, an attending physician from Johns Hopkins, and a colleague of the famous William Osler. He left my backstory alone, probably not sure what to say or who would believe it.

After Neil's introduction, I began my address. "To the distinguished staff of the Vienna hospital, you may know that I was born an orphan in the Vienna Foundlings and Orphans Home. My mother was a physician in this hospital, an obstetrician who died of childbed fever after I was born. My life has been blessed by my always being at the right place, having great mentors, and having an affinity for science. The rumors are true that I was with Pasteur when he developed and provided the germ theory; with Lister when he changed the history of surgery through antisepsis; and with Koch when he proved that certain bacteria, germs, or animalcules, whatever you choose to call them, cause specific disease. But I am not here to talk about myself or any of these other men with whom I worked closely.

"In 1847, the year my mother died, many thousands of other women had also died from a disease called childbed fever. There were two obstetrical wards back then, one run by physicians, the other by midwives. In the physician ward there were ten times as many postpartum deaths than in the midwife ward. The Vienna hospital, as you know, was never a backward hospital but one with new ideas and excellent doctors, many of whom were at the forefront of new knowledge.

"After years of study, Ignaz Semmelweis, working with my mother and with Drs. Skoda and Ferdinand von Hebra, came to the ghastly conclusion that these women were dying from the hands of their beloved doctors, doctors who often would go from patient to patient, surgery to surgery, and even to and from autopsy rooms with hands that were unclean. When Ignaz put a chlorine sink in the middle of the ward and required physicians to wash their hands, the deaths of these women and the disease puerperal fever were extinguished.

"But your predecessors at this hospital—and perhaps some of you are here now in your twilight years—could not believe this doctrine. They disbelieved not because they reviewed the science, the facts that Semmelweis had carefully gathered, but because they chose not to do so. Who wanted to believe that their own hands had caused the deaths of patients? So Semmelweis was insulted and labeled a Hungarian foreigner who did not speak well and who was a danger to the profession of medicine. Lesser men might have moved on— some of his group did move on—but he was not one to give up. He fought for his ideas in writing, in conferences around Europe, and right here in this room, but he was not believed. He died a broken man in an insane asylum.

"I do not need to provide evidence for the Semmelweis doctrine. Dr. Joseph Spath, a fierce opponent of the doctrine, later published in the winter of 1861, fourteen years after Semmelweis's paper, that 18 percent of women in the obstetrical wards contracted childbed fever, and 13 percent died from the disease, whereas the disease occurred very rarely, in 1 percent, among those who gave birth on the street. And eventually, even Semmelweis's worst critics, those who had persecuted him without mercy, came to agree that something on physicians' hands was causing the puerperal deaths.

"Isaac Newton once said, 'I can see farther because I stand on the shoulders of the giants who came before me.' Pasteur, Lister, and Koch stood on the shoulders of Ignaz Semmelweis. They found what was on the hands of those physicians: microbes, deadly microbes, able to be seen under the microscope, able to be grown in culture.

"I have been told that I have the ability to see things in the future that others may not see. I see in the future Ignaz Semmelweis's picture on the walls of the great universities of the world, alongside those of Pasteur, Koch, and Lister. I see Semmelweis recognized as the man who saved millions of human lives with one of the greatest, most important discoveries the world has known. He was a genius, a courageous scientist, albeit a tragic hero. And I see the medical school of his country carrying his name someday, his face on coins and stamps around the world. But most importantly, I see great scientists of the future from all countries standing up for their discoveries based on science and willing to defend their conclusions despite political or cultural conflict.

"I did not know Semmelweis—I met him once when I was twelve years old—but I have come to you today, members of the staff of the Vienna hospital, to honor his name and work and to ask you to do the same."

And so my first speech ever was well received, with applause, with a standing ovation. I had reached another milestone in my life's work.

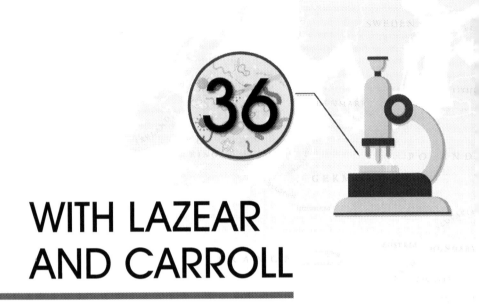

WITH LAZEAR
AND CARROLL

Returning to Baltimore, I settled into a life of academic medicine and caring for patients, mostly those who lived in poverty, which contributed to most of their health problems. I continued to assist Dr. Osler in writing *The Principles and Practice of Medicine*, concentrating on the chapters that discussed disease caused by some type of animalcule: bacteria, parasites, and those with no known cause. I thought this comprehensive book might well become the bible for internal medicine diagnosis.

Of special interest at Johns Hopkins was the disease called malaria. Our laboratory meetings had included Osler, Welch, Lazear, Carroll, Walter Reed, and me. Osler and the group had fallen behind the times on this disease. Several pathologists, experts in blood disease more than in microbes, had reported that there appeared to be some type of parasite right there in the white blood cells of victims. Osler at first doubted their findings, including those of one of our own pathologists, William Councilman. Osler had not seen such parasites, describing only some types of specks within red blood cells. So we all started looking more carefully at samples. We spent many hours looking at the stained blood samples of patients with the symptoms of malaria, those who had periodic fever and sweats. I became an expert at looking at red blood cells, something I had not cultivated an interest in before. I was used to looking through a microscope lens for hours on end, probably more so than others, and this did pay off. Of most interest was what appeared to be flagellated bodies—parasites with a tail—in the red blood cells.

I shared these findings with Carroll and Lazear. Carroll still wore his US Army uniform but was enthusiastic to be assigned to the Welch laboratory. He planned to become a professor in the new Army Medical School.

Lazear, just out of medical school, was particularly excited to study malaria. Jesse and I had become friends. He was much younger than I, in his early thirties, a graduate of Johns Hopkins and Columbia Medical School who also had done a short stint at the Pasteur Institute. He, too, was in the US Army and expected to stay in academic medicine. Like me, Lazear had come to place great value on research but also on teaching young medical students. He was especially interested in comparing blood smears of malaria patients with their specific symptoms. Those with the flagellated parasites seemed to have much more severe and multisystem disease. Lazear also had seen some patients with a more severe disease but with some similar signs and symptoms, those with yellow fever. These patients did not have positive blood smears, and the disease was much more mysterious and life-threatening in them.

Osler did eventually become convinced, after an exhaustive and continued review of blood smears, that a parasite was causing malaria. Even more importantly, he endorsed the use of quinine to treat malaria based on the careful follow-up with patients who were treated. Osler would not easily believe in any therapy unless he had good clinical evidence of its efficacy. On many occasions, he told us of his disappointment in treating infectious diseases, especially tuberculosis, for which he helped disprove the tuberculin treatment. But also, he had not found any progress in the treatment of pneumonia, typhoid fever, anthrax, or skin infections, now called erysipelas. Osler also began to doubt even antipyretics, drugs to reduce fever, wondering if perhaps fever itself might be of benefit to the patient.

To Lazear and me, Osler's endorsement of quinine was greatly encouraging. If a specific drug could help cure malaria, why not a drug for each and every microbe that caused a specific disease? We hoped to see such drugs in our lifetime.

Lazear was one of the few with whom I had shared my story, the whole story including my loss of Adrienne in Alexandria. Lazear had just married, and he was able to understand not just my loss but also the sacrifice made by Adrienne and her colleague.

"Jacob, to give one's life for this war against microbes is such a noble cause. Perhaps that can be some solace to your sorrow."

Lazear, Carroll, and Reed all would move on to teach at other medical schools: George Washington and the US Army Medical School. I missed our sessions on malaria, but I continued a fulfilling career in academic medicine.

A new member of the Welch and Osler team joined the lab, and I was quite surprised to see her, sitting right next to me and looking at some slides. She wore a white coat and had a large amount of black hair, all in a bun above her head.

Attempting to be polite, I asked her, "Are you a new lab assistant?"

"No, I am not," she said.

"A nurse?"

"No, sir, I am not a nurse."

"I am Jacob, a physician on the staff here, and I am pleased to meet you."

"I am Dorothy Mabel Reed, a medical student, soon to graduate."

"I apologize for assuming that you were a nurse here."

"Well, that is not the first time that has happened to me. There were thirteen of us women in the first class, but most of us could not stand the constant bias and abuse. But not only have I made it; I also have been chosen as an intern for next year."

"On what service?"

"On the Osler service."

"So Dr. Osler has been supportive of the new women students?"

"Not at first. On my first day of school, he told me to go home, just as I was walking in the door."

"That does not sound like the man I know."

"He genuinely believed women should be at home—be good wives and mothers. Why would he think differently than almost the entire male dean community and faculty around the country? Even still, only a few schools will take women at all. But I know that my resilience has changed Dr. Osler. He told me he will support me in every way as an intern, and I know that I will need his support. And you, Jacob? What do you think about women physicians?"

I needed to take a breath at this point in this surprise encounter and to be sure that I did not suddenly embarrass myself through tears. "Dorothy Mabel Reed, my mother was one of the first women physicians in Vienna, a physician and scientist who died of childbed fever at the Vienna General Hospital after giving birth to me."

Now Miss Reed was on the defensive. "Well, I suppose then I have a friend in you," she said, hiding her shock.

"Yes, you do. You know, some have said that I have a way of seeing the future. Well, I see more women than men as physicians in this country someday. I think they have the right attitude and the right aequanimitas, as Osler would say. And to change the subject, what are you studying?"

"I am looking at the pathology of Hodgkin's disease, establishing the difference between the pathology of lymphoma and that of tuberculosis. It is an area of interest to Osler and Welch, and I have been working with a pathologist from Austria, Dr. Carl Sternberg—I guess one of your countrymen."

"And your findings?"

"We are looking at a very particular cell, a giant cell with more than one nucleus. It is seen only in those with Hodgkin's disease, not with tuberculosis. We will be publishing our findings."

"My advice: always take credit for what you have discovered. I would have liked to have done that a bit more myself."

"Meaning?"

"Well, call it the Reed-Sternberg cell. Then people will always remember you. And Dorothy, if you or any other woman intern needs the support of an attending physician, you can always call on me. I think my mother would be proud of me for lending such support."

In 1900, I was fifty-two years of age and content with a life at the Johns Hopkins Medical School and Hospital that had brought me great meaning and healing. Life changed again when I received a letter from Jesse Lazear, from whom I had not heard for about three years.

Jacob,

> *You may know that I have been assigned as an assistant surgeon at the Columbia Barracks in Quemados, Cuba. I am here with Dr. Carroll and under the direction of Dr. Walter Reed. A young Cuban, Dr. Agramonte, is also working with us. We are part of a commission studying the cause and transmission of yellow fever. Yellow fever has killed thousands of Cubans, but it is killing our soldiers stationed here as well, including many of the officers under General Leonard Wood. The disease, as you know, presents with fever, vomiting, and liver failure, resulting in jaundice and bloody vomitus. We have no cure and no known microbe.*
>
> *Jacob, the public health ignorance is striking. The people here are in a kind of panic, burning their clothes or even burning their houses. They distrust each other and look for someone to blame. No one wants to go anywhere near their neighbors. Transmission of the disease is odd. It comes in waves, leaves in colder weather. Our nurses are so frightened to care for the sick soldiers, but in fact they never seem to get sick while on the job.*

Dr. Reed is in charge of a hospital for the care of yellow fever patients. He personifies Osler's aequanimitas: calm, levelheaded, clear-thinking always. But we are losing young, previously healthy patients and soldiers every day. We have all done the microscopy, but we find absolutely nothing, no microbe and no red blood cell findings, and there is plenty of tissue to review. Autopsy specimens of liver have not been helpful.

Jacob, frankly, we could use some help. A civilian scientist and expert in microbes would become an important part of our team. I would never ask anyone else, but I know that you have the experience and commitment to see this as an opportunity. If you do decide to come to Cuba, I can make all necessary arrangements.

DEATH IN CUBA

Havana, Cuba, was hot and muggy. I had been fatigued by the flight, which had been sponsored by the US Army, and then drenched by rain upon arrival. I was driven to the Columbia Barracks, where fourteen hundred military troops resided, part of a poorly publicized Spanish-American war. We were eight miles from the city of Havana, according to my driver, but I saw only lush foliage and palm trees blowing savagely in the wind as we drove to the base. There had been a few casualties from war but many from yellow fever. There were multiple tents, a makeshift hospital, and a laboratory.

In the laboratory, I met with my two former colleagues, Drs. Carroll and Lazear, and was introduced to Dr. Aristides Agramonte, a young Cuban physician trained in the United States and interested in infectious disease, especially yellow fever.

Dr. Reed had been in Cuba but recently had been called back to the United States, where, to the surprise of the group, he had been asked to return to Washington to report on typhus in the US Army.

Agramonte began to explain to me the challenge that I had somehow agreed to undertake with this group. He had been in Cuba longer than the others. I had to just glance at Jesse Lazear to know that all was not well. We were no longer in the safety of a medical school environment. I interrupted Agramonte briefly and impulsively asked Jesse about his wife.

"Jacob, thank you for asking. It is my wife and two children now," he said with a sardonic grin. "Well, of course they worry about me."

Agramonte continued, "When Major Reed came to Cuba, I had the day before established a yellow fever hospital, under tents, attended by men who had already recovered and were immune to the disease. We stood in the men's quarters with several hundred beds spread out in one large room. Already, several soldiers had died from the disease, and their beds were removed. Jacob, I want you to know that one of the men who died was a soldier prisoner newly admitted to prison, even though he'd had symptoms of the yellow jack beforehand. He was in very close contact with seven other prisoners and died after seven days, but no other prisoner became infected. We also know that the soldiers who wash the bedsheets and the clothes of those infected, even those who have died, also have not become infected."

"I remember when I was at the Vienna orphanage and found that the children with typhus also were infected by lice. But those without lice did not become infected even when close to others."

"Yes," said Dr. Carroll, "that is a model we have been exploring."

"So you think that this is a disease spread by insects or some environmental cause that is more common outside the barracks than inside?"

"Yes, we have met with a Dr. Carlos Finlay of Havana. For years he has suspected that mosquitoes may be causing this disease. He has been met with disbelief and ridicule. Nevertheless, we consider mosquito transmission a possibility."

Jesse spoke with a nervousness that was just not characteristic. "James and Aristides are working with the autopsied cases, doing the microscopy, and looking at blood smears for parasites. I am working with the eggs of mosquitoes that Dr. Finlay has given us. I am trying to see if the mosquitoes can be infected from the clothes of the soldiers—a long shot, I know. Jacob, you may remember hearing of a Dr. Rush at the University of Pennsylvania. He wrote that during the yellow fever outbreak in Philadelphia, he was quite sure there was a preponderance of mosquitoes in the city that year.

"I have also carefully put mosquitoes in a glass tube covered with a cotton swab, much like one of your bacterial cultures. We tip the glass tube and add some blood from an infected soldier to see if the mosquitoes die on contact with the blood. They do not."

"I would have suspected that they would not," I interjected.

"We know that many of our soldiers during this time have been bitten by mosquitoes and have not become ill."

"Dr. Jacob," said Aristides, "I was born in Cuba and trained in the United States but have recently returned and have had numerous mosquito bites without any illness similar to the yellow jack."

"James, I would like to work with you doing the microscopy," I said, "with immersion oil and staining materials."

"Yes, we have the best microscopes, just no photomicrographs."

The four of us slept in a tent on cots, separated from the soldiers and the laboratory. I had trouble sleeping, remembering those days in Alexandria. I had always wondered if Adrienne and Thullier and my own team had really understood the risks we'd subjected ourselves to. But I also felt exhilarated that I was now back in the fight against the microbes that I had willfully declared war against since the age of twelve. We all must take risks and find those things that were worth fighting for. This was my war and where I needed to be.

In the morning, I reviewed the blood smears of those infected with yellow fever, plus the vomitus, the diarrheal stool, and even samples of liver from autopsies. There was no evidence of a bacterial agent causing this disease—no large Gram-positive rod, no clusters of grapelike bacteria, no chainlike streptococci or cholera-like vibrios. There were no malarial parasites.

"As you know, this doesn't mean there is no microbe, just not one we can see," I said to Jesse.

"Like smallpox," said Jesse Lazear.

"Yes," I agreed, "or like measles or, as I have heard from Pasteur, like rabies."

"Jacob, come with me to the wards and see what you think of the patients' history and physicals," said Jesse.

We walked to a large tent filled with twenty cots bearing patients in various stages of illness.

"Dr. Jacob, this is Mr. Garcia from Havana."

I touched Mr. Garcia's shoulder. He nodded to me. He was having some difficulty speaking.

"Mr. Garcia, do you have any pain?"

"Yes, Doctor. All my muscles ache, and my stomach hurts on the right side. Light hurts my eyes."

I examined the patient. His skin was jaundiced, yellow under good light. His liver was enlarged and could be felt on the right side, several inches below the lower rib. My fingers, curled under the rib cage on the left side, touched the spleen tip as he took a deep breath. He was awake but lethargic.

"Mr. Garcia, do you know where you are?"

"I dream about being at the lake near my home, fishing."

"Mr. Garcia, were you bitten by a mosquito?"

He forced a smile. "Who hasn't been?"

A nearby patient offered more history. "That poor guy is hallucinating at night. Thinks he is with his girlfriend."

There were other patients sitting on their cots, reading or speaking to each other. Some had mild eye discoloration and fever but didn't appear that sick. This yellow fever could be severe or very mild.

We all met back at the laboratory.

"What is the evidence for mosquito transmission?" I asked. "Let's review this again."

"Dr. Finlay of Havana has suspected this for years," said Dr. Carroll.

"But why?" I asked.

"It occurs during times when the mosquitoes are everywhere and goes away when they are gone."

"Yes," said Jesse, "and the same was suspected in Philadelphia."

"Still, that does not prove a causal relationship."

Dr. Agramonte said again, "I have lived in Cuba for years with the mosquitoes and have never gotten sick."

"Perhaps you were only mildly ill and never thought much about it."

"I was never yellow—have had white sclera all my life."

"But it is true that this disease is not being transmitted from one patient to another?"

"Yes, it does not seem to be. A sick soldier comes into a barrack that has not had the disease, and no one seems to get it from the new admission."

"So the idea is a mosquito bites someone who has yellow fever, picks up the microbe, then bites another person, who gets sick."

"Or people go outside in warm weather, and the air itself is toxic," suggested Agramonte.

"Miasma? Toxic air?" asked Jesse.

"Perhaps," said Agramonte.

"No, Aristides, I don't think so. Miasma is an obsolete theory. It was not correct for childbed fever, not for cholera, not for tuberculosis."

"Jacob," said Jesse, "you remember when you swallowed the sour milk?"

"I do."

"And you showed that there were bacteria in the milk, and the bacteria likely made you sick?"

"Yes. Pasteur was not pleased with me."

I think we all had the idea at about the same time. We had no animals to work with, and our soldiers had already suffered enough from this disease. It would not be right to make any more of the soldiers ill.

"It needs to be us, to prove to the world that this disease is caused by mosquitoes," said Dr. Carroll. "Or if it is not, then we must start to look elsewhere."

"Aristides," I asked, "if mosquitoes were the culprit, what would be the significance?"

"We could eradicate them, get rid of all the places where they breed, find the best toxins against them."

"I will go first," said Dr. Carroll.

"Count me in as well," said Jesse Lazear. "Just don't let my wife know."

I said, "I, too, am in, of course. Isn't this the dramatic fight against microbes that I have always been ready for?" Adrienne had not feared her work in Alexandria.

Aristides was not in but assured us that he would be there to care for us, if necessary.

James Carroll asked, "Just how would this experiment be done?"

"Only one way—let the mosquitoes feed on the yellow fever patients, collect the mosquitoes in test tubes, and let them bite us as they emerge from the tubes."

James Carroll said, "Let me go first. We will take turns, separated by a few days in time."

"Why the separation?" I asked.

"Well, we don't all want to get sick at the same time."

For the record—and the army kept good records—no matter how wild, outrageous, foolhardy, or valiant this experiment might sound, it did take place. The yellow fever patients helped us find mosquitoes on their ward. Blocking mosquitoes from escaping their test tubes was a great way to get bitten. This exciting experiment, the Cuban mosquito experiment, was on. We each took our turn at being bitten by a test tube–trapped mosquito.

About six days later, we found Dr. Carroll quietly examining his own blood, but of course finding no microbes or malarial parasites. He told us he had a cold, but his eyes were bloodshot, and his face was flushed. He settled on the lounge in the laboratory but before long said that he had to go to bed. That Jesse and I suddenly felt panic-stricken was not logical. Hadn't this been the hypothesis of the experiment—that mosquitoes might spread yellow fever?

Dr. Carroll developed fever, at first low-grade but then raging. He would almost collapse every time he tried to get up. Again, his delirium, his abnormal mental status, was characteristic of others with yellow fever. But his eyes were more a muddy brown than a true yellow, and his skin was not jaundiced. Instead of turning yellow, instead of vomiting blood, he slowly gained strength.

But days later, Lazear, my true friend, the husband and father of two, the one among us who had the most to lose, began to feel out of sorts. He stayed in his quarters all day and complained of a chill that night. Aristides and I looked after him with a sense of doom. We notified his family that he was ill but being well cared for. He slept well, but the next day, when we saw him in the morning, his eyes were yellow. On the same day, Dr. Carroll fortunately was up and about. He would be fine, and we hoped Jesse would be as well.

But that was not to be. The agony of suspense that I had experienced in Alexandria had returned to my life. For seven days, Dr. Carroll, Aristides, and I followed Jesse's downhill course, which was especially torturous with a loving wife and children waiting for our every contact. Lazear was going in and out of delirium but would tell us in his lucid moments that we were saving the world from the mosquito and from some tiny microbe. He asked me to come close to him and told me that I had given him courage and had inspired him to join the war against microbes.

Seeing Jesse so sick had left me more drained and fatigued than I had ever remembered being. But I stayed up at night, cooling his forehead with wet towels. We agreed to use quinine. We knew that it worked for malaria, so why not try it?

As Jesse became more ill, I felt both physically ill and emotionally destroyed. I thought about all the losses, the people that I'd cared about most, the mother I had never known, and now Jesse.

As Jesse became weaker, I realized that in fact I had not thought much about myself, other than my mental distress. But on the fourth day of Jesse's illness, in my own reflection I saw that my eyes were brownish-yellow, and my nausea was not the emotional kind. I was becoming ill.

By the following day, Jesse Lazear and I shared cots side by side, with Dr. Carroll and Dr. Agramonte looking after us.

Jesse, in what seemed like a great effort, raised his head from his cot and looked toward me with eyes sunken and face now clearly yellow. "Jacob, we are heroes, are we not?" And those were Dr. Jesse Lazear's last words.

I went in and out of sleep. I heard Dr. Carroll ask me if I had any next of kin, and I responded that I did not.

I realized that I was becoming confused and that I was vomiting black material, a poor prognostic sign in yellow fever. Aristides asked me who Adrienne was, as that was the name I was calling in my delirium.

Osler had told us that death came softly to the great majority of patients, and few actually died in fear. That seemed to be true as I was not afraid and not regretful.

In my last conversation with Aristides, he recalled my dream from the night before. "Jacob, you kept repeating the same words: 'The window is open. I left the window in the lab open. And the wind has blown through the lab onto the animalcule plates, killing all the bacteria on the plate. Let them know.'"

Then I called for James Carroll, who came to my cot tearfully, probably much like the obstetricians had come to see my mother.

"James, should I not survive, I have in my desk drawer the story of my search for the animalcules. It may inspire others in what will be one of mankind's greatest challenges."

OBITUARY

D
r. Jacob Pfleger died on September 25, 1900, in Quemados, Cuba, of yellow fever. Dr. Jesse Lazear, a US Army sergeant, also died of yellow fever on the same day. Both were studying the yellow fever epidemic in Cuba.

Jacob was born in Vienna, Austria, in 1848 and raised in a Vienna orphanage. He is said to have been a laboratory assistant for Louis Pasteur, Joseph Lister, and Robert Koch. He graduated from medical school at the University of Pennsylvania in 1884 and worked as a resident and faculty member at the new Johns Hopkins medical school. He had no known family members.

AFTERWORD

T he era of childbed fever ended with the understanding that it was a bacterial infection that could be prevented by hand washing. The medical school in Budapest is now named the Semmelweis University School of Medicine. Stamps and coins from many countries have Semmelweis's face on them.

Dr. Robert Koch received the Nobel Prize in 1905 for his work in identifying the causes of anthrax and tuberculosis and proving that bacteria could cause disease.

Dr. Louis Pasteur won the Nobel Prize in 1907 for his work to establish the germ theory.

Joseph Lister changed the way surgery was performed all over the world, although his carbolic acid technique is no longer used.

Gerhard Armauer Hansen identified the bacteria that caused leprosy in 1873, a mycobacterium in the same family as tuberculosis.

A dormitory at Johns Hopkins has been named for Dr. Jesse Lazear. Dr. Walter Reed stated, "I lament his loss more than words can tell, but his death was not in vain. His name will live in the history of those who benefited humanity."

A secondary school in France is named for the martyr Dr. Louis Thullier.

William Osler was the chair of medicine at Johns Hopkins from 1888 to 1904. During that time, he revolutionized medical education with bedside teaching and ushered in the era of scientific thinking. His book *The Principles and Practice of Medicine* is the most comprehensive textbook of medicine ever written by one author.

Mosquito control has wiped out yellow fever in most countries. A virus was isolated as a cause of yellow fever in 1923.

Rabies, measles, and smallpox also have a viral etiology and can be identified by electron microscopy.

In 1923, Alexander Fleming discovered penicillium, and the antibiotic era began. His discovery was an accident in that the penicillium mold entered his laboratory through an open window and killed bacteria on a culture plate.

In the twenty-first century, thousands of hospitalized patients have died from staphylococcal infection caused by physicians who did not wash their hands.

Jacob, Jacob's mother Marie, Neil, Luc, Pierre, and Adrienne are fictional characters.

Alexander Fleming knew of his countryman Dr. Lister, but it is not known that he ever met Lister or Pasteur as a young student or attended the Pasteur party.

Koch found bacterial growth on a potato, but it was not known to be a potato that Gertrude had saved for her pets.

All the cases seen with Lister and Koch come from the actual files of real patients.

There is some evidence that Joseph Lister did speak with Semmelweis while visiting Vienna on his honeymoon, but this visit is disputed by some.

Pasteur did visit Napoleon III and dined at his castle. Lister did remove an abscess from the queen and accidently sprayed carbolic acid in her face.

DEDICATION

This book is dedicated to all the following people:
To Ignaz Semmelweis and all those scientists whose work was never appreciated in their lifetime.
To the models of scientific excellence: Pasteur, Koch, and Lister.
To all those Jacobs who contributed to the great discoveries of the early infectious disease era, but whose names will never be known.
To Lazear and Thullier, martyrs in the battle against microbes.
To the hundreds of healthcare workers who have died fighting COVID-19 as the war against microbes continues.
And a special dedication to all physicians who wash their hands after seeing each patient.

Thanks to those who reviewed the manuscript prior to publication: Dr. Rial Rolfe, Dr. Kate Holder, Dr. Charles Bryan, Dr. Sergey Kunkov, Shirley Berk, Dr. Justin Berk., and Dr. Sarah Ahmed.

ABOUT THE
AUTHOR

D r. Steven Berk is an infectious disease specialist and dean of the Texas Tech Health Sciences Center School of Medicine.

Printed in the United States
by Baker & Taylor Publisher Services